FIELD STUDY

ALSO BY RACHEL SEIFFERT

The Dark Room

FIELD STUDY

RACHEL SEIFFERT

PANTHEON BOOKS, NEW YORK

Library of Congress Cataloging-in-Publication Data
Seiffert, Rachel.
Field study / Rachel Seiffert.
p.   cm.
Contents: Field study—Reach—Tentsmuir sands—Dog leg
lane—Blue—Architect—The late spring—The crossing—
Francis John Jones—Dimitroff—Second best.
ISBN 0-375-42259-5
I.Title.

PR6069.E345F54 2004   823'.92—dc22   2003066364

www.pantheonbooks.com

Book design by M. Kristen Bearse

Printed in the United States of America
First American Edition
2   4   6   8   9   7   5   3   1

CONTENTS

FIELD STUDY

FIELD STUDY

Summer and the third day of Martin's field study. Morning, and he is parked at the side of the track, looking out over the rye he will walk through shortly to reach the river. For two days he has been alone, gathering his mud and water samples, but not today.

A boy shouts and sings in the field. His young mother carries him piggyback through the rye. Martin hears their voices, thin through the open window of his car. He keeps still. Watching, waiting for them to pass.

The woman's legs are hidden in the tall stalks of the crop and the boy's legs are skinny. He is too big to be carried comfortably, and mother and son giggle as she struggles on through the rye. The boy wears too-large trainers, huge and white, and they hang heavy at his mother's sides. Brushing the ears of rye as she walks, bumping at her thighs as she jogs an unsteady step or two. Then swinging out wide as she spins on the spot: whirling, stumbling around and around. Twice, three times, four times, laughing, lurching as the boy screams delight on her back.

They fall to the ground and Martin can't see them

anymore. Just the rye and the tops of the trees beyond: where the field slopes down and the river starts its wide arc around the town. Three days Martin has been here. Only another four days to cover the area, pull enough data together for his semester paper, already overdue. The young woman and her child have gone. Martin climbs out of the car, gathers his bags, and locks the doors.

This river begins in the high mountains Martin cannot see but knows lie due south of where he stands. Once it passes the coal and industry of the foothills, it runs almost due west into these flat farming lands, cutting a course through the shallow valley on which his Ph.D. studies are centered. Past the town where he is staying and on through the provincial capital, until it finally mouths in the wide flows which mark the border between Martin's country and the one he is now in. Not a significant stretch of water historically, commercially, not even especially pretty. But a cause for concern nonetheless: here, and even more so in Martin's country, linking as it does a chemical plant on the eastern side of the border with a major population center to the west.

Martin has a camera, notebooks, and vials. Some for river water, others for river mud. Back in the town, in his room at the guesthouse, he has chemicals and a microscope. More vials and dishes. The first two days' samples, still to be analyzed, a laptop on which to record his results.

The dark uneven arc of the trees is visible for miles,

marking the path of the river through the yellow-dry countryside. The harvest this year will be early and poor. Drought, and so the water level of the river is low, but the trees along its banks are still full of new growth, thick with leaves, the air beneath them moist.

Martin drinks the first coffee of the day from his flask, by the water's edge. The river has steep banks, and roots grow in twisted detours down its rocky sides. He has moved steadily west along the river since the beginning of the week, covering about a kilometer each day, with a two-kilometer gap in between. Up until now, the water has been clear, but here it is thick with long fronds of weed. Martin spreads a waterproof liner on the flat rock, lays out vials and spoons in rows. He writes up the labels while he drinks his second coffee, then pulls on his long waterproof gloves. Beyond the branches, the field shimmers yellow-white and the sun is strong; under the trees, Martin is cool. Counting, measuring, writing, photographing. Long sample spoon scratching river grit against the glass of the vials.

Late morning and hot now, even under the trees. The water at this point in the river is almost deep enough to swim. Martin lays out his vials, spoons, and labels for the third time that morning. Wonders a moment or two what it would be like to lie down in the lazy current, the soft weed. Touches his gloved fingertips to the surface and counts up all the toxic substances he will test his samples for later. He rolls up his trouser legs as high as they will go before he pulls on the waders, enjoys the cool pressure of the water against the rubber against his skin as he moves carefully out to about midstream. The weed here is at its thickest, and Martin decides to take a sample of that, too. The protective gauntlets make it difficult to get a grip, but Martin manages to pull one plant from the riverbed with its root system still reasonably intact. He stands awhile, feeling the current tug its way around his legs, watching the fingers of weed slowly folding over the gap he has made. Ahead is a sudden dip, a small waterfall that Martin had noted yesterday evening on the map. The noise of the cascade is loud, held in close by the dense green avenue of trees. Martin wades forward and when he stops again, he hears voices, a laugh-scream.

The bushes grow dense across the top of the drop, but Martin can just see through the leaves: young mother and son, swimming in the pool hollowed out by the waterfall. They are close. He can see the boy take a mouthful of water and spray it at his mother as she swims around the small pool. Can see the mud between her toes when she climbs out and stands on the rock at the water's edge. The long black-green weed stuck to her thigh. She is not naked, but her underwear is pale, pink-white like her skin, and Martin can also see the darker wet of nipples and pubic hair. He turns quickly and wades back to the bank, weed sample held carefully in gauntleted hands.

He stands for a moment by his bags, then pulls off the waders, pulls on his shoes again. He will walk round them, take a detour across the fields, and they will have no cause to see him. He has gathered enough here already, after all. The pool and waterfall need not fall within his every-hundred-meters remit. No problem.

Martin sleeps an hour when he gets back to the guesthouse. Open window providing an occasional breeze from the small back court and a smell of bread from the kitchen. When he wakes the sun has passed over the top of the building and his room is pleasantly cool and dim.

He works for an hour or two on the first day's mud and water vials, and what he finds confirms his hypothesis. Everything within normal boundaries, except one particular metal, present in far higher concentrations than one should expect.

His fingers start to itch as he parcels up a selection of samples to send back to the university lab for confirmation. He knows this is psychosomatic, that he has always been careful to wear protection: doesn't even think that poisoning with this metal is likely to produce such a reaction. He includes the weed sample in his parcel, with instructions that a section be sent on to botany, and a photocopy of the map, with the collection sites clearly marked. In the post office, his lips and the skin around his nostrils burn, and so despite his reasoning, he allows himself another shower before he goes down to eat an early dinner in the guesthouse café.

―――――――

The boy from the stream is sitting on one of the high stools at the bar, doing his homework, and the waitress who brings Martin his soup is his mother. She wishes him a good appetite in one of the few phrases he understands in this country, and when Martin thanks her using a couple of words picked up on his last visit, he thinks she looks pleased.

Martin watches her son while he eats. Remembers the fountain of river water the boy aimed at his mother, wonders how much he swallowed, if they swim there regularly, how many years they might have done this for. Martin thinks he looks healthy enough, perhaps a little underweight.

His mother brings Martin a glass of wine with his main course, and when he tries to explain that he didn't order it, she just puts her finger to her lips and winks. She is thin, too, but she looks strong; broad shoulders and palms, long fingers, wide nails. She pulls her hands behind her back, and Martin is aware now that he has been staring. He lowers his eyes to his plate, watches her through his lashes as she moves on to the next table. Notes: *Good posture, thick hair.* But Martin reasons while he eats that such poisons can take years to make their presence felt; nothing for a decade or two, then suddenly tumors and shortness of breath in middle age.

The woman is sitting at the bar with her son when Martin finishes his meal. She is smoking a cigarette and checking through his maths. The boy watches as Martin walks toward them, kicking his trainers against the high legs of his bar stool.

— I'm sorry. I don't really speak enough of your language. But I wanted to tell you something.

The woman looks up from her son's exercise book and blinks as Martin speaks. He stops a moment, waits to see if she understands, if she will say something, but after a small smile and a small frown, she just nods and turns away from him, back to her son. At first Martin thinks they are talking about him, and that they might still respond, but the seconds pass and the boy and his mother keep talking, and then Martin can't remember how long he has been standing there looking at the back of her head, so he looks away. Sees his tall reflection in the mirror behind the bar. One hand, *left, no right*, moving up to cover his large forehead, *sunburned*, and red hair.

— What do you want to say to my mother?

The boy speaks Martin's language. He shrugs when Martin looks at him. Martin lets his hand drop back down to his side.

— Oh, okay. Okay, good. Can you translate for me, then?

The boy shrugs again, which Martin takes to be assent, and so he starts to explain. About the river, how he saw them swimming in the morning and he didn't want to

9

disturb them, but that he has been thinking about it again this evening. And then Martin stops talking because he sees that the boy is frowning.

— Should I start again?

— You were watching my mother swimming.

— No.

The boy whispers to his mother, who flushes and then puts her hand over her mouth and laughs.

— No. No, that's not right.

Martin shakes his head again, holds both hands up, but it is loud, the woman's laughter in the quiet café, and the other two customers look up from their meals.

— I was not watching. Tell her I was not watching. I was taking samples from the river, that's all. I'm a scientist. And I think you should know that it is polluted. The river is dirty and you really shouldn't swim there. That's all. Now please tell your mother.

The young woman keeps laughing while Martin speaks, and though he avoids looking in the mirror again, he can feel the blush making his sunburn itch, the pulse in his throat. The boy watches him a second or two, lips moving, not speaking. Martin thinks the boy doesn't believe him.

— You could get sick. The river will make you sick. I just thought you should know. Okay?

Martin is angry now. With the suspicious boy, his laughing mother. He counts out enough to pay for his meal, including the wine. Leaves it on the table without a tip and goes to his room.

In the morning, a man serves Martin his breakfast, but before he leaves for the river again, the young mother comes into the café, pushing her son in front of her. She speaks in a low whisper to the boy, who translates for Martin in a monotone.

— My mother says she is sorry. We are both sorry. That she is Ewa, I am Jacek. She says you should tell me about the river so I can tell her.

Martin is still annoyed when he gets back from the river in the afternoon. Doesn't expect the woman and her boy to stick to their appointment, still hasn't analyzed day two and three's samples, half hopes they won't turn up. But when he comes downstairs after his shower, he finds them waiting for him in the café as arranged.

The boy helps Martin spread out his maps, asks if he can boot up the laptop. His mother murmurs something, and her son sighs.

— She says I should say please. Please.

— It's okay.

Martin shows them the path of the river from the mountains to the border and where the chemical plant lies, almost a hundred kilometers upstream from the town. Amongst his papers, he finds images of what the metal he has found in the river looks like, its chemical structure and symbol, and he tells them its common name. He says that as far as they know, the body cannot break it down, so it stores it, usually in the liver. He speaks a sentence at a time and lets the boy translate. Shows them the graphs he has plotted on his computer. Waits while the boy stumbles over his grammar, watches his mother listening, thinks: *Jacek and Ewa.*

— Where do you come from?

Ewa speaks in Martin's language, points at the map. Martin looks at her, and Jacek clears his throat.

— I am teaching her.

Martin smiles. He shows them where he is studying and then, a little farther to the west, the city where he was born. And then Jacek starts to calculate how many kilometers it is from Martin's university to the border and from the border to the town. Martin asks Ewa:

— How old is he?

— Nearly eleven.

He nods. Thinks she must have been very young when she got pregnant.

— He's just about bilingual already.

An exaggeration, a silly thing to say, and Martin can see in Ewa's eyes that she knows it, but she doesn't contradict him.

— School. He is good student. Also good teacher.

She smiles and Martin is glad that they came today, Ewa and her son. Pushes last night's laughter to the back of his mind. Sees that Ewa's smile is wide and warm and that her tongue shows pink behind her teeth.

Day five and Martin works his way along the river again. The hot fields are empty, the road quiet. The water here is wider, deeper; flies dance above the surface.

Midmorning and Jacek crashes through the under-growth.

— Martin! There you are. I am here.

Martin looks up from the water, startled. He nods, then he doesn't know what to say to the boy, so he carries on working. Jacek watches him awhile, and then pulls off his trainers, rolls up his trousers, picks up a vial.

— No! You shouldn't come in.

— I can help you. You work faster when I can pass them to you.

— Shouldn't you be at school?

Jacek frowns.

— Does your mother know you are here?

— She don't mind.

Martin thinks a moment.

— We don't know enough yet about this metal, you see. It's too much of a risk.

Jacek avoids eye contact, rubs his bare ankles.

— You really can't help me without boots and gloves, Jacek. I only have one pair of each. I'm sorry.

An hour later the boy is back with pink washing-up gloves and a pair of outsize rubber boots, soles caked in mud. He holds up a bag of apples.

— For you. From my mother.

In the evening the café is crowded and Ewa is busy; another waitress brings Martin his dinner. His table is near the bar, where Jacek is doing his homework again. New vocabulary, and he asks Martin to correct his spelling. Ewa makes a detour past his table on her way to the kitchen.

— Thank you.

— No problem.

He scratches his sunburn, stops. Feels huge at the small table after she has gone.

Jacek brings his mother with him on day six. Ewa stands at the water's edge while her son changes into his boots and washing-up gloves. Midday already, and the sky is clear, the sun high. Martin has sweat patches under his arms, on his back. He watches Ewa hold the front of her T-shirt away from her chest, and then flap it back and forth to get cool air at the hot skin beneath. He sees yellow pollen on her shoes, the hem of her skirt, damp hair at her temples.

They work for a while, and Jacek asks questions which Martin answers. Ewa says very little. She crouches on the bank and looks at the water. Lids down, lips drawn together, arms wrapped around her shins. When Martin says it's time to move downstream, a hundred meters, Jacek says he wants to come with him and Ewa says she will go home.

Jacek watches Martin watching his mother as she wades through the long grass back to the road.

— She used to swim here with my Tata, I think.

— Your father?

Martin tries to remember a wedding ring. Sees Ewa's strong palms, her long fingers.

— He is in your country.

— Oh?

— He is illegal. Too much problems at the border, so he don't come home.

Martin watches Jacek as they unpack the bags again. Fair with freckles. Narrow lips, pale eyes, broad nose. A good-looking boy, but not at all like his mother.

Day seven and Martin doesn't go to the river. After breakfast he sets up his computer, a new graph template, and plots the data from days two and three. Both agree with day one's graph, with Martin's predictions, and he starts sketching out a structure for his argument, writes a first-draft conclusion. The sample results should have come back from the university yesterday, including the mud and weed from day four, which would speed up Martin's analysis. He goes downstairs to the small office mid-morning to check for faxes again, but the guesthouse is quiet, café closed, reception deserted. Sunday. So there won't be anybody at the labs, either, but Martin walks out to the phone boxes in the town square anyway.

Jacek hammers on the glass.

— Where were you?

— Wait.

Martin holds up one finger, but the phone just keeps ringing out at the other end. Jacek peels his pink gloves off while Martin leaves a message on the lab answer phone. The boy cups his hands around his eyes, presses them up to the glass, watching him. It is stifling inside the phone box and Jacek's hands leave a sweaty streak on the pane outside.

When Martin opens the door, Jacek has his fists on his hips. Rubber boots on the paving stones beside him.

— Why didn't you come?

— I've finished. I only need to do a couple more tests.

— Oh.

Jacek picks up his boots and falls into step with Martin. The sun is strong and they walk together on the shady side of the narrow street which leads back up to the guesthouse.

— I'm going home tomorrow.

— Tomorrow?

He looks up at Martin for a second or two, then turns heel and runs.

Martin sleeps in the afternoon and is woken by the land-lady's husband with a message.

— Is it from the university?

— No. From my wife's sister.

Martin stares at the man. Eyes unfocused, face damp with heat and sleep.

— From Ewa. Jacek's mother. She works here. My wife's sister.

— Oh, yes. Yes, sorry.

— She says you should come to her house. She will cook you something to eat this evening. To say thank you.

Martin showers and sits down at his computer again but finds he can't work. Looks out at the birds instead, washing in a puddle on the flat roof of the building opposite. The concrete is mossy and Martin wonders where the water came from. He has been here a week and it's been in the mid-eighties straight through and hasn't rained once. The skin on his back is damp again, and under his arms, and he thinks he hasn't anything clean to wear this evening, so he takes a T-shirt down the hall with him and

17

washes it in the bathroom, lays it out on his windowsill to dry.

It is still slightly damp when he goes out to find Ewa's. Bottle of wine bought from the guesthouse bar under one arm, map and address on a scrap of paper from the land-lady's husband. There is a slight breeze and the T-shirt is cool against his skin. He catches sight of himself in the bakery window as he passes, pushes his hair down over his forehead a little as he turns the corner. An involun-tary gesture he hopes nobody saw.

Jacek opens the door.

— You're early!

— Sorry.

He leads Martin up the stairs, two at a time, cartons of cigarettes and cake mix piled high along one wall. The narrow entrance hall of Ewa's flat is similarly crowded: disposable nappies, tuna fish, toothbrushes in different shades, pink and green and yellow. Jacek sees Martin looking at the boxes.

— The man we rent from. He keep things here, we pay him not so much. Every week is something new coming for him to sell.

A table stands in the middle of the room, a wardrobe in the corner. Mattress leaned up against the wall and draped with a sheet. The window is open and the radio on. Martin recognizes the song, a current hit, but can't understand what the announcer says afterward. He goes into the kitchen, where Ewa is chopping and Jacek stirring.

— Can I help?

— No!

Ewa pours him a glass of wine and pushes him out into the bedroom–dining room again.

— Five minutes.

The wind is blowing into town from the river, and Martin can hear church bells ringing out the evening service.

They eat, Martin and Ewa smiling and nodding, Jacek concentrating on his food, not worried by the silence.

— Jacek, can you ask your mother to tell me a little about the town, please?

The boy looks up with his mouth full; Martin swallows.

— I know very little. I would like to know.

It is not true. He knows what she tells him already, what the boy translates for her about the nine churches, the resistance during the war and occupation, the failed collectivization of the fruit growers during the communist era.

— There was a jam factory here when she was my age. Everybody was working there, or they were farmers. Apricots, pears, apples, and I don't know how you say those small ones. Berries?

Martin asks about the communist years.

— You want to hear about no food and unhappiness, yes?

Martin rubs his sunburn, and Ewa slaps her son's hands.

— Jacek! Sorry. I don't understand him, but I see he was bad. You translate only, yes? Yes?

Ewa points at her son and then pours them all more wine, offers to make Martin some tea.

— The way we drink it here.

Jacek's translation is sulky, sleepy. Black, in a glass so you can see the leaves floating. Boiling water, hot glass with no handles so your fingerprints get smooth and hard from the holding. Martin looks at the tips of his fingers; Ewa smiles.

— I didn't know your sister owns the guesthouse.

— Yes.

Ewa smiles, Jacek yawns.

— She gives my mother work.

— And her husband?

— Tadeusz?

— Uncle Tadeusz does no work.

— Sh! Not true.

Ewa speaks more herself now, interrupts her son's translations. She tells him her brother-in-law is a plumber. That he put his faith in the church. Her explanations are ungrammatical, sometimes nonsensical, but Martin enjoys listening to her. She says that they built new houses a year or two after the elections, a whole row, right in the center. New times, new buildings. Flats above, shop spaces below. Brick, solid, good windows. And Tadeusz put in all the pipes, toilets, baths, taps, sinks. He got a loan to pay for all the materials. Copper piping and ceramics, imported from the West. He had the houses blessed when they were finished but not yet painted. The priest came and threw his holy water around the empty rooms and Tadeusz was so proud. She remembers the wet, dark spots on the pink-red plasterwork, that it was a hot day, and that the dark spots left white marks behind when they dried.

— He never got paid, Tadeusz, and he cries often now.

Each time he defaults on his loan, and the houses are still empty. A while ago there was new graffiti on the wall of the last one in the row: Send the nuns abroad and the priests to the moon.

Ewa looks at Jacek, who isn't listening anymore, eyes half closed, head propped in his hands. She whispers to Martin:

— I think Tadeusz write that.

Martin feels her breath on his neck as she speaks, can smell wine and soap mixed.

— My sister, she wanted that Jacek and me should live with her. After Piotr left.

— Your husband?

Ewa doesn't answer, her eyes are unfocused.

— I couldn't. Not live with Tadeusz. He's not a bad man, but so much bitterness.

Martin is drunk and so is Ewa.

— I don't want my son be bitter, you see. I want him to like his life, this town, his country.

Martin nods.

— There is not so much here now, but I show him places, take him to the river.

Ewa sighs. They sit with the breeze from the open window on their bright cheeks and Jacek has his head on the tablecloth, asleep.

— I don't make him be at school this week. I think he can't swim in the river now, but it is good that he speaks with you. Has some nice time, learns someone new. More than in a classroom.

Ewa smiles into the middle distance and Martin looks at her. Only half a meter between them, the corner of the table, knees almost touching underneath.

He leans toward her. But Ewa catches him.

— No.

One hand on each of his shoulders, she holds him at arm's length. Martin blinks.

An empty wine glass rolls on the table. Ewa shakes her head.

— Sorry, no.

She smiles and then Martin sits back in his chair again, sunburn itching, sweat prickling in his scalp.

He doesn't look at her, and for a minute or so they sit in silence. Jacek's even breathing in the room and the church bells sounding again outside. When Martin looks up, Ewa is blinking, smiling at him.

— I am sorry.

She rights the glass on the table, then covers her mouth with her hand and laughs.

In the morning there is a fax from the department lab. Martin has a hangover, asks for coffee and water to be sent up to his room. His eyes skim the figures, cannot settle. He boots up the laptop, plots the lab's figures onto his graph, though he already sees the disparity between the last set of results and his predictions. Days one and two show serious levels of contamination in mud and water, and correspond with Martin's own data. Day three's samples, however, are almost low enough to be considered clear.

Martin sits on the narrow bed awhile, trying to decide if he is relieved or disappointed. The weedy water, the pool under the waterfall: *Clean. As good as.* But the premise of his paper: *Void.* His headache is bad, the day hot already, the shame of yesterday evening still fresh. Martin presses the heels of his palms against his eyes.

He wants to go home, he needs to get dressed. He goes to the bathroom, where the window is open, the air much cooler than in his room. He stands under the shower a long time, warm flow on face and shoulders taking the edge off his headache, filling his ears, closing his eyes, re-placing Ewa and her laughter with water falling on tile.

The room he returns to is strewn with papers and clothes. Martin works his way round it methodically, fold-ing and sorting into piles. Before he packs, he checks through the lab technician's tidy columns once more, notes the memo at the end of fax: The weed sample has been sent on to botany.

On the way downstairs, he reasons with himself: If the weed results are interesting, he can propose to further in-vestigate the river fauna in the conclusion to his paper. Over breakfast, he thinks he could propose a joint ven-ture with botany, perhaps. Something to please the de-partment. Zoology might even be interested: The weed may be thriving, but crowding other species out. At the very least, it is good news for Ewa. She is not working this morning, but Martin thinks he will leave a note for her, tell her it's okay to take Jacek swimming again. He finishes his roll. Thinks he made a mess of the field study, the week in general, but there are still ways to make amends.

Martin stands in the narrow reception hall with his bags, sees Ewa happy by the waterfall while her sister calculates his bill. Then he remembers how sad she looked the day she came with Jacek to the river, and he is shocked at the satisfaction the memory gives him.

There is paper on the counter in front of him. He has a pencil in his back pocket, but he doesn't get it out. He pays and picks up his bags. While he loads up the car he tells himself it is too soon to know for certain. He has yet to test all his samples, examine all the possibilities; swimming at the waterfall could still be dangerous.

On the road out of town, he sees Ewa's hand over her mouth, her eyes pressed shut, Jacek woken by her laughter and staring at him.

At the border, the road runs parallel with the river for a kilometer or so, and the traffic moves slowly. To his right, trees grow tall along the riverbanks, and in his rearview mirror Martin can see the rest of the country spread out behind him, dry and flat. His chest is tight with shame, but the border guard is waving him through now, and he is driving on again.

REACH

Wednesday, and Kim's mother goes up to the school for parents' evening.

— She's doing badly, then.

— Well, no, not exactly. She can read and write. Quite well for a seven-year-old, as it happens.

Her daughter's class teacher pushes Kim's report around on the desk with her fingertips, and Alice waits for her to pull the words together.

— She's just not an easy child to reach, Mrs. Bell.

Home is the end house of the terrace above the seafront. From her bedroom window, Kim can see over the rooftops to the old pier and, beyond it, the last curve of sand before the headland. Seagulls hover on thermals, suspended, and Kim watches them at the window, swaying, waiting. From here she will see her mother when she comes home from the school.

In the door and then chopping, no sitting down between and no hello either. But this is not unusual. Kim's description of her mother in one of her schoolbooks: She always cooks with her coat on.

Kim waits after her mother has passed along the path beneath her windowsill to the back door and the kitchen. Face still pressed to the wall, and so still hidden from the street below, Kim listens awhile to the pot and pan noises, then goes downstairs to find Alice. Early evening, getting dark, her mother is working by the blue light of the grill flame, chops spitting underneath. Kim stands in the doorway a minute or so, but Alice does not turn. An evening like any other: potato peelings on the counter, mother's back at the sink. Kim wonders briefly if she got the day right, if Alice has been to the parents' evening after all, but decides against mentioning it. Joins her brother in the sitting room instead, watches TV with Joseph until dinner.

If she's staying, Alice will take her coat off and eat with her children. Tonight, she has a cup of tea and makes sure the washing up is under way before she heads off out to work again. A reminder of bedtimes and a brisk kiss each on her way to the door. This too is normal, so Kim breathes a little easier, dries the plates slowly that Joseph washes fast. Watches the familiar sight of her mother's back receding down the garden path. She can close her eyes and see Alice making her way down the hill to the seafront. Keys gripped in her right hand, left holding her collar together against the wind.

Kim's eyes are sore tonight, scratchy, her lids heavy. She keeps them closed, keeps her mind's eye on her mother a little longer. Imagines the sea flat behind Alice as she opens the salon door, surface skimmed into ripples by the wind. She knows her mother chose the shop for its view across the beach, along the seafront. Has heard her telling the customers, watched her polish the wide glass window clean of rain and salt. Alice plays no music in her salon, she does not talk much. There is calm when she cuts and sets hair. In the summer with the door open and the sea air. In the winter with the hum of the dryers and the wide window misted against the dark afternoons.

Kim opens her eyes again at the kitchen window, her mother long gone, brother back in front of the television. She dries her hands on the damp tea towel, flicks the last crumbs of dinner off the kitchen table. Kim tries to rest her forehead on the cool surface, but can't, her neck stiff, resisting, caught somehow by her shoulders. The days before the parents' evening have been edgy, and she can't relax now, not sure what to do with all the worry.

When Alice is asked about her business, she says she makes a decent living for her family. Margins are tight with debts like hers, but she has no gaps in her appointment book to speak of, few concerns to raise with her accountant.

When Alice thinks about her daughter, as she does

this evening, she sees her pale eyes and paler hair, the solid flesh of her face with its closed, impassive expression. Stubby thumbs sucked white and soft and drawn into tight, damp fists.

Alice has long fingers and strong nails: neat ovals without cuticles. She does them last thing before she leaves the salon, after the work is done. Alone with her thoughts and files. Rubbing the cream in, hand over hand over hand.

She didn't argue with what the teacher said this afternoon. *Not an easy child.* Alice has heard those words before now: from different sources, in different disguises, so many times she has come to expect them. Would never say so, but she agrees.

With Joseph it was simple: Love arrived with him. Fury when the midwife carried him away from her across the delivery room to be washed and weighed. Kim was early. Only a few weeks after Frank had gone. Gas and air, and Alice kept telling the midwife she wasn't ready for the baby, but she came anyway. No tears and not much pain either. And then it took Alice years to get used to her: her rare smiles, her uncooperative arms and legs.

Alice hears the pigeons shuffling in the eaves above the doorway as she locks up. The soft, quivering noise they make in their throats. The water behind her is calm, just a slight breeze coming in across the sands. Breaking up the surface a little, touching her cheek as she turns the key in the lock and up the street toward home.

———

Thursday, and Kim is ill.

She vomits once at school. A pile of sawdust and a smell in the corridor. Again when she gets home. Joseph heats the dinner Alice has left in the fridge for them, and when Kim throws up a third time, he phones the shop.

— Can you come home now, Mum?

— Run her a bath and put her to bed, love. Please. I'll not be late. Make sure she drinks something.

Joseph does as he is told, and his sister is silent, compliant. When Alice comes home it is dark and Kim is running a fever: dry heat and then sudden sweats which glue her pale hair to her forehead.

Friday morning, Kim can't stand up to walk to the toilet, and so when she needs to throw up again, her mother finds her crawling out into the bright hall.

— No school for you, then.

An unwieldy deadweight with limbs. Alice carries her daughter to the bathroom.

Cold black tea. Chalky taste of the aspirin mashed into jam and eaten with a teaspoon. Alice is home for fifteen minutes at lunchtime, keeps her coat on. Stands her daughter naked by the radiator, washes her down with a flannel and hot water in a red plastic bowl. Kneeling next to her clammy body, its awkward joints and dimples, soft belly.

Kim's eyes are half closed and she sways as Alice works. Hot cloth on face and neck, round ears, down spine, between toes and fingers. Skin turning cool where the flannel has been.

Kim lies in new pajamas when Alice leaves for work again. Under new sheets and tucked blankets, curtains drawn against the day. The slats of the bunk above her shift, and birds' eyes peep from the mattress. Beaks and wings. Kim calls for her mum, but she's gone now, back down the road. The hair-spray smell of Alice left with her, and Kim is alone with the birds again. They fly out from between the slats, gray wings beating the hot air against her cheeks.

Alice always hoped it would come. Read about it in the leaflets she got from the midwives and the library. You will not always bond with your baby immediately, but this is normal and no cause for worry.

Kim arrived and Alice had two to care for. Frank gone and only one of her: didn't seem nearly enough. Joseph was four then and she would pick him up from nursery school early. To feel his hand holding her skirt as they walked home along the seafront, to have his arms fold around her neck when she lifted him up.

Alice tried holding Kim after her evening bottle, after Joseph was asleep and they could have some quiet time together, like it said in the leaflets. But it was hard and sometimes it frightened her: sitting with her baby and still feeling so little.

Red-brown spots gather in the afternoon. On the soles of Kim's feet, behind her ears, inside her eyelids. Joseph sees them when the doctor shines his torch in his sister's dark bedroom. He pulls the girl's eyelids down with his thumbs.

— I'll need to use your telephone. Call an ambulance and your mother.

Joseph tells Kim later that they drove away with the siren on, but Kim remembers silence inside the ambulance. Looking at her mother and then following Alice's gaze to the trees and lampposts passing. The strip of world visible through the slit of clear window above the milk glass in the doors.

Alice Bell's girl had meningitis and nearly died.

The customers in the salon ask concerned questions, and Alice gets a call from the health visitor, too. The woman has a good look at the clean hall, the tidy kitchen Alice leads her to. The grass in the garden is long, falls this way and that, but Alice is sure that everything else is in good order. Thinks she recognizes the health visitor, too: that she has maybe cut her hair before.

Alice gets more leaflets from her. Is told about the

tumbler test: Roll a glass against the rash, she says. Alice thanks the woman, but thinks it's not really any good to her, this information. It's happened now, over; Kim will be home again soon.

The house is quiet after the health visitor leaves. Small. Alice sweeps her leaflets off the kitchen table, dumps them in the bin on the front on her way back to the salon.

Kim has scars. A tiny, round wound in the small of her back, where they tapped the fluid from her spine. And one on the back of her hand from the drip: skin and vein still slightly raised, puncture mark already healing, fading with the black-turning-yellow bruise. She has fine, white scratch lines on the soles of her feet, too, but these are more memory than reality. Pin-tip traces to check for sensation, pricks in the tops of her toes that drew blood drops, which later become blood spots on the hospital sheets.

The real scar is at her throat. Tracheotomy. Kim can't say the word, but this is where her fingers go at night in her hospital bed, and when she wakes. To feel the way the skin is pulled over, small folds overlapping and grown together. Like melted plastic, the beaker which fell in on itself when Joseph left it on the stove. At first the hairy ends of the stitches are there too. Six black bristles for Kim's fingertips to brush against under the dressing: to investigate in the bathroom mirror when no one else is there to be looking. One hand on the wheely drip, the other pushing herself up on the sink, closer to the long, clean mirror and the gray-pink pucker of skin in her reflection.

Kim is back at home now, back at school. Weeks have passed already, but Alice still sees the first days in the hospital with her daughter. The pictures come at her from nowhere. When she is doing the books, while she is cutting, shopping, walking, on her way home.

From her bedroom window, Kim watches her mother in the dusk light, coming up the road. She walks with her coat unbuttoned and sometimes she stops, head down, hands deep in her pockets. Stays like that for a minute or two on the pavement before walking on.

The nurses held Kim's body curled and still and Alice watched. Daughter's spine turned toward her, small feet pulled up below her bum. Brown iodine swirled onto her skin, and then her toes splayed as the needle went in: five separate soft pads on each foot, reaching.

They had a room free for Alice down the hall, but she stayed in the chair by her daughter's bed and didn't sleep much. Awake when Kim's temperature rose again and she swallowed her tongue. The doctors drew the curtain round the bed and the fitting girl while they worked. So Alice couldn't see what they were doing any longer but still she didn't move. Stayed put, listening, while they made the hole for the tube in her daughter's neck, and took her temperature down with wet sheets around her legs. No one asked Alice to leave, and she sat in the chair, shoes off, coat on, pulled tight around her chest.

Kim has headaches, too.

Joseph watches while his sister ties the belt round her head. One of Granddad's old ones. Big buckle, cracked leather: round her forehead, over her temples. He pulls it tight for her and then she lies down, head under the blankets, nose showing. Brows pulled into a frown by the belt, jaw clenching, neck held taut against the pain.

Kim's drinks have to be warm because her teeth feel everything, and she is clumsy. Legs bruised from falls and corners, clothes stained colorful by spills. Kim has no sense of edges these days: where a glass can be placed safely, where her body can pass without damage. She creates noise and mess, and the mumbling speech that the doctor said should improve quickly takes weeks to go away.

The school calls Alice in again. No parents' evening this time: a meeting with Kim's class teacher and headmistress, attendance register open on the desk between them.

— When does Kim leave the house, Mrs. Bell?

— Quarter to nine. With her brother.

— Every morning?

Alice nods, doesn't tell them that she leaves the house at eight-twenty to open the salon. Thinks they are doubtless capable of working that one out. She reminds them.

— My daughter has been very ill.

— Yes.

They are writing things down and Alice is remembering again. That Kim couldn't stop herself looking at her tracheotomy wound. That the peeled ends of the dressing curled up off her neck, giving her away, gathering dust like magnets, tacky traces on her skin turning black. Alice visited her at visiting time, whispered: It'll get infected. She smiled when she said it. Didn't want to tell her daughter off; just to tell her. Let her know that she had noticed. That she understood it, her curiosity.

Kim looked at her. Skin under her eyes flushing. Hands moving up to cover the dressing. Alice didn't know what that meant: whether her daughter was surprised or pleased or angry.

— Kim is what we call On Report now, Mrs. Bell.

— She could have died.

— Yes.

They blink at her across the desk. Sympathetic, insistent.

— I'm afraid her attendance record has to improve.

Kim finds different places to spend her days. Sometimes
the coast path over the headland, where the wind cuts
into her legs. Sometimes the burnt stubble of the fields
inland, where she flies her kites made out of plastic bags.
Most days it is the beach, though, where she lies down
under the old pier. On her back on the cracking shingle,
waves at her feet, seawall behind her. Sodden wood, salt,
seaweed, and litter.

Above her, she can see the gulls' flapping battles through
the gappy planks of the old walkway. Lies still, watching
the starlings fly their swooping arcs around the splintered columns and rails. Cloud and wind over the water.
Storm of black beak and wing reeling above her head.

Alice shuts the salon early and is home before her children. Joseph acts as though it is normal for his mother to
open the door for him; Kim steps into the hallway, clutch-
ing her schoolbag as if it were proof of something, tell-
tale damp of the day in her clothes and hair. Joseph slips
upstairs to his bedroom, Kim stays silent, eyes on the
wallpaper while Alice asks her where she has been and
why. She watches Kim's face for a reaction but cannot
read anything from her daughter's expression.

— Whatever. You'll be leaving the house with me
from now on.

— No.

Later Alice goes over the scene again. In bed, light out,

eyes open. Feels something closing down, tight around her ribs. Remembers the screaming battles they had when Kim was three, four, five: doesn't want to repeat those years again. Her daughter smelled of sea and air this afternoon, it filled the corridor. Alice didn't know what to do, what to say, so she said nothing. An almost eight-year-old stranger standing in front of her. Mouth open, breath passing audibly over her small, wet teeth.

Kim doesn't know it, but the school keeps close tabs on her. Her teachers know she comes for registration and then dodges out of the gate behind the playing fields. They don't confront her; instead they call her mother and then Alice hangs up the phone in the back room of the salon, behind the closed curtain, under the noise of the dryers, and cries.

Alice doesn't know it, but some mornings her daughter comes down to the front. The smell leads her there: hot air, warm skin and hair, shampoo. She doesn't go in; instead she watches her mother's face at the salon window. Eyes and cheekbones amongst the reflections. Blank sky, cold sea, ragged palms. Her mother's eyes blinking, face not moving. Lampposts with lights strung between, rocking in the breeze.

Another Wednesday, another week or two later, and Kim stands in the salon doorway. Alice has had the phone call already. Knows her daughter hasn't been to school, didn't expect her to show up here. The rain slides down the windowpane, and through the open shop door, she can hear it singing in the drains.

Alice takes her daughter's coat from her, sits her down in an empty chair. The salon is quiet and Kim spends the next few minutes watching her mother working in the mirror. She sees that Alice doesn't look at her, only out the window, or down at her fingers, turning gray hair around the pastel shades of the plastic rollers, pink and yellow and green. Her mother's cheeks are flushed, lips drawn in, and the skin around her eyes pulled taut.

When Alice steps over to her, Kim looks away. Sees the old lady's eyes on them, under the dryer. Alice knows she is watching them, too. Has felt her customers observing her ever since Kim was ill, has grown accustomed to the scrutiny. She stands behind her daughter now. A second or two passes, and she finds herself still there. Not shouting, not angry. Just looking at the slope of her daughter's shoulders, the nape of her neck, her sodden hair.

Alice gets a clean towel from the shelves at the back and then plugs in a dryer, sets to work. At first Kim watches the rain, the gulls fighting on the rail outside, but soon she closes her eyes. Feels the pressure of her mother's fingers, how strong her hands are, how warm the air is, the low noise of the dryer.

TENTSMUIR SANDS

The boy is carsick. After his journey backward along the motorway and then through the pines. In the back of the long family car, between the cool box and the beach towels, staring at the white stripes on black tarmac receding, the corners and trees of the sandy track to the beach.

Parked under high pines on needles and springy ground, doors opened to the sound of waves and smell of outside. The dunes give way under the feet of the boy's mother, father, his two brothers, his sister. He is the youngest and his hands are clasped by his parents on the walk to the beach from the car. One on either side, they pull his arms high above his head.

The family reaches the top of the rise together, all six stopping a moment at the highest point of the rolling dune. The wind is blowing in off the sea and pastes their summer clothes to their skin. The mother and father swing their youngest up over the tough grass tufts. Small feet lifting off the shifting sands, the lurching-belly feeling a happy one now, nausea driven back to the car by the wind, the wet salt, and tree smell out here.

Before them are the three stripes of sky, sea, and sand. Powder blue, slate, and then brown. Indian summer, weekday, they are alone. Save a kite flier and two dog walkers plus collie, barking at the retreating surf. Snout snaps shut in silence and the sound reaches the family, their youngest son, late. Carried on detours by the wind, across the flat sands up the rise of the dune to their ears.

They scaled it on their toes and descend now, heels sinking deep into the pale gold slope. The mother is breathless, father frowning, and they let go of their youngest boy, attention turned fully to their ungainly struggle down the dune with the picnic box. The older boys throw themselves forward and land on the beach first, rolling and kicking. Laughing and throwing fists of sand after each other, running away to the water.

The sister, the eldest, walks slowly, keeps a few paces between herself and her parents. With her face turned out to sea, she avoids the sight of her father's bald spot, her mother's wide-legged walk, the fact that they link arms, pointing out birds to one another, hopping at the water's edge. She keeps her own arms folded square across her chest.

Her youngest brother skips awhile somewhere behind her, then runs full pelt past her and past their parents out into the middle of the wide sands.

The father spreads the towels out in front of the windbreaker and the mother lies down. Almost on one side, knees bent, one foot planted firmly on the ground. She sleeps briefly, chest rising and falling with her breath. Breasts large again, belly facing out to sea, a huge, firm curve under the wide material of her dress. The breeze blows a dusting of sand across her strong feet, their high arches and prominent veins. They run dark blue under her pale skin, from the tops of her feet to her calves, the backs of her knees.

The sister lays her towel a couple of meters away and reads. Earphones leaking tinny whispers back to her little brother, who sits by their parents, shoveling sand from hand to hand. His father unpacks a carton of juice for himself, for the boy.

— Shall we go and find your brothers, then?

His small son sucks red drink up through the straw and nods. His wife sits up, halfway, propped on her elbows.

— You stay here, love. Rest.

He puts a hand on her belly, a kiss on the top of her head.

The father walks barefooted, trousers rolled up. His legs are white and his toes pink, soft from their sock casing. He leaves heavy prints on the wet sand, which soften and fill with water after he has passed.

— I've brought you an extra man.

The boy's brothers stand in the shallows and scowl.

— Come on. Play something where he can join in.

And they do for a while, but it is no fun and so soon turns into piggy in the middle, with a new rule. If the ball goes in the water, piggy has to fetch it, and before long the small boy's shorts are wet through. After that it just makes sense to throw him in a little deeper, especially because he laughs such a lot when they swing him. One holding his shoulders, the other his legs.

The water is cold, though, and salty. Catches in his throat and brings back the sick feeling of this morning in the car. He cries, and so they have to take him back up the beach to their mother, who frowns and says do they have to be so rough with him and they may as well stay here now and eat some lunch.

The youngest boy is undressed and wrapped in a large towel, hair rubbed spiky and half dry by a smaller one. He eats his sandwich slowly, crust first, sitting close to the bulging stripes of the windbreaker, silently regarding the frayed tops of its wooden posts.

His father spreads the boy's shorts and T-shirt out on the sand to dry, weighted down with stones from the tide line, corners flapping in the breeze. He takes off his own shirt for his son to wear, sleeves turned all the way up in fat rolls, tails trailing to the boy's ankles. The father sits in his vest and gives his children riddles to solve over their sandwiches. They roll their eyes, but venture answers all the same. He is delighted when they solve them, even more so when he can explain the solutions to them. Using gestures for emphasis, and enigmatic diagrams drawn with his fingers in the sand.

— Mum, can I go down there?

The youngest son stands in his father's shirt and points down the beach to the far headland. His father's riddles mean nothing to him, his explanations even less. His mother blinks, sleepy again.

— What's down there, love?

He shrugs.

— I want to see.

— Maybe in a bit, sweetheart. Have you finished your lunch?

He sighs, kicks his feet about in the sand. His father and brothers have moved a little way from the patch of towels, are drawing in the sand with sticks now. But what the picture is of, the youngest boy can't make out.

— I'll go with him.

The sister is embarrassed by her father's behavior, by her brothers, even though there is no one else on the beach now to see them. Her mother smiles, tired, grateful.

— Thank you, love. I'll join you in a while, then.

The girl walks just fast enough so that her little brother has to skip occasionally to keep up. A slim pack of ten is pulled out of her waistband once they have got enough beach between them and their parents. Flick-flick noise of the cigarette lighter repeating behind her hand, she crouches down, gets the small boy to shield her from the wind.

— Pretend you've found a shell.

She instructs and he mimes dutifully, picking up nothing and placing it on her outstretched hand. Her other is held stiff to her side, cigarette hidden from distant parents' eyes by her body, smoke kicked this way and that, quickly invisible in the wind. A swift, checking glance back to the parents, and sister stands again.

They walk together. Near the water's edge, where the sand is hard and rippled and the last soft reaches of the waves wash over their steps. The boy fishes seaweed from the shallows and his sister pops its leathery bulges for him with her fingernails. He finds long, flat stripes floating a little farther along, yellow-brown and tough as plastic, which he drags back up onto the beach to where his sister is sitting, arms wrapped round her knees.

She curls the long stripes round to form her initials against the sand.

Her brother recognizes the letters:

— Kuh, suh.

— Yes. *C-S*. That's me.

He laughs and runs back to the water for more stripes, which she forms into more letters, and then decorates both sets of initials with a few pebbles and shells.

— Is that me?

The boy points at the second pair. A *P* and a *D*, carefully laid. His sister laughs.

— No!

— Oh.

Her brother looks down at the letters and blinks, surprised. His sister sighs. Kneels down and lays the rubbery stripes out new. She smiles at him.

— Buh, suh. That's you.

They walk on, dune and pine on their left, sea on their

right, specks of parents and brothers far behind. Ahead of them the beach is cut in two by a stream, a dark strip of sand and silt mixed. Mossy stones sit wet in the shallow flow.

— Will we go across?

The boy's sister wrinkles her nose. Beyond lies the headland and gray rock. A wide sandbank out in the water.

— Nah.

She gets out her cigarettes again, and her brother squats down next to her, looks out at the low rise of the sandbank, almost level with the sea.

— What are those dark things?

He points out to the sandbank.

— Rocks.

— They're moving.

— No.

— They are so.

Some of the dark shapes on the sandbank move, others are still. The brother and sister watch silently for a while, and then the little boy stands.

— Look!

He runs down toward the water, to a small mound on the bank of the stream, a small shape lying there, out of reach of the sea. He gestures to his sister as he runs.

— Come on!

But when he gets there, he recoils. Small hands fly to his face. Stock still and silent by the shape by the stream.

His sister frowns and stands, walks down the sand to her brother, to the thing he is looking at.

It is a young seal. Lying almost on one side, soft belly facing out to sea, sand built up in a drift against its back.

— Dead, kiddo.

His sister smokes and squints, crinkling up the skin around her eyes. Spaces between her freckles pink from sun and wind. The boy looks down at the seal again. Wet ends of his father's shirt blowing against his legs, small rounds of his knees showing through the graying cotton. He turns his back to the sea, and stands so the young seal is protected from the wind. Looks round, over his shoulder, searching out the dark shapes on the sandbank, their slow, distant movements.

— Shit.

His sister drives the end of her cigarette deep into the sand at her feet, cups her hands over her mouth, and tests her breath. The boy follows her gaze and sees his mother. Advancing slowly, belly first toward them across the wide beach. She calls something to them, but he can't make it out, and her hair is whipped across her mouth.

When she gets to them, she is out of breath and the hair at her neck sweat-damp. She stops.

— Oh.

Then takes the last couple of steps to her children, the dead seal next to them.

— Oh dear.

She puts a hand on her son's head, but he can't take his

47

gaze off the place where the seal's eye used to be. Tattered hole in the side of its head. Pelt still fuzzy. Flipper and belly dusted with fine white grains.

His mother hugs the boy to her legs, draws her daughter toward her and kisses her hair. Then frowns.

The boy pulls away from his mother, turns his attention out to sea. His mother takes hold of his sister's hand, sniffs it, and then drops it again, eyes turned hard. Her daughter blinks and pulls her lips into a tight line. Flush creeping from below her T-shirt to her neck. She pulls the cigarette packet out of her shorts and lays it on her mother's outstretched palm.

The boy is watching the dark shapes again. The creatures roll on the far bank, their noise, somewhere between bark and wail, carries in snatches across the wind-broken surface of the water to the beach. One or two are swimming. Camouflaged. Brown-dark skins against gray-dark sea, but the boy can just about make them out. Heads reaching up out of the water, slanted shoulders. Snouts turned to one side to allow closer scrutiny of the figures on the shore with one eye. They are still. Like they are standing. Rising and falling gently with the waves.

— Mum. Do they know he's dead?

His mother looks out at the water.

— I don't know, love. Maybe.

— Are they sad?

— I suppose they might be.

He looks down again at the half-buried seal body.

— Will I die before you, Mum?

— Oh sweetheart, I shouldn't think so.

— What about Celie?

His sister frowns under his mother's eyes.

— No, I hope she will live longer than me.

— But one of us will die first?

— Yes, I suppose one of us will.

— And the rest of us will be sad?

— Yes, I'm afraid so.

The boy frowns, his eyes dark now, looking out at the watching seals, their sandbank being claimed by the encroaching tide.

— Can't we just die all together?

His mother blinks. She strokes his hair.

— Well, no. I'm afraid that's very unlikely.

The rest of the afternoon is spent building castles. Big enough for the boy to stand in, with turrets made by his father and mother and shell and seaweed adornments collected by his sister. His brothers dig a moat, which fills with foaming water when the tide reaches them. Smoothing the castle walls, washing off one or two of the lower shells that decorate the family's fortress. Their father takes a picture of them all, kneeling in order of height in front of their creation, their mother smiling, standing to one side. The low sun throws long shadows in front of them, and turns the sea behind them gold-white.

It is cold now and they pack up, walk back over the dune together, out of the wind into the silent pines and the car. The hatchback hisses open and the boy climbs inside.

First the dunes disappear and then the trees. It grows dark and they are back on the big road. The tires roar below the boy on the tarmac and he rests his head on the pile of towels beside him, still damp, still smelling of sun. His skin feels tight and warm, and he listens to his brothers and sister murmuring on the backseat behind him.

There is sand inside his shoes, between his toes, in the pockets of his clothes. Small white dustings of it in the gray carpet of the car boot. A crunch in the sandwich his mother gave him for the journey home.

He sees the dead seal when he closes his eyes. At night now, but the sand is still pale and the wind still blowing. The eyes blinking at him over the water are large and black and wet, and the noise from the sandbank sounds like crying.

DIMITROFF

My father is not part of my life.

Her husband is silent a moment, then continues:

— The man is not a father. He is an irrelevance.

And she says:

— If he's so irrelevant, why do you get so worked up about him?

And her husband sighs and lies still on the sofa next to her, and she feels the breath move his chest up and down, up and down, and his heart beating faster than normal.

Hannah has met her father-in-law only once, eight years ago. Before the heart problems started and the strokes. He came over for their wedding in his customary black beret and coat. His first trip abroad since the wall came down. His first time beyond the now-tattered iron curtain. Opposed, he announced at the reception, to what he called Jochen's American dream; disappointed, he continued, that his son should have been so taken in.

— West Germany was bad enough, but the U.S.A. I don't think I will ever understand.

He smiled while he said it, but nobody laughed because it was not at all clear whether he was joking.

The first stroke happened two years later and Jochen flew to Berlin. When his father was well enough, he drove him across Germany to Karl's place, Jochen's older brother. To Frankfurt am Main: temple of West German commerce. It was supposed to be a temporary solution, a period of convalescence. Six years later he is still there, and now the situation is critical.

— He never lifted a finger for us, Hannah. My mother did everything.

Jochen repeats this phrase like a mantra. Most mornings, and sometimes also when they get into bed. A defensive reaction, Hannah thinks, to his father's descent into old age, his neediness. Not necessarily representative of Jochen's underlying feelings. Her own parents are both still young, not even retired yet, and she knows she cannot predict how well she will respond when their time comes. But still, Hannah is unsettled by this new, bitter side to her husband.

It is a time of many phone calls. Long distance brothers talking Brooklyn to Frankfurt. Diagnoses, updates, endless debates. Safety first or dignity, home care or nursing home, where will the money come from, what do you mean his insurance won't pay for that, so why didn't he get private cover, damn him?

— But we have money, Jochen. Karl has money. It's not a problem.

— Jesus Christ, Hannah. It's not about the fucking money.

Jochen swears like an American, only sounds like a German when he gets annoyed. Flat vowels, sharp consonants. It makes Hannah want to smile, but she is shocked, too. Almost a decade together, and she has never seen him so angry.

They go upstate for the weekend, get away from the phone.

— My mother left him. A couple of years later we left East Germany.

Jochen drives, and Hannah sits in the back with the twins sleeping one on either side of her, strapped into their bright and padded seats. There are long silences, just the engine, the tires on the road, and Hannah waits for Jochen to talk again, watching the freeway stretch off in front of them, the back of her husband's head.

— I was five. So Karl was nine or ten.

Part of Hannah is glad this is happening. Not that her father-in-law is ill, and that her husband is unhappy, but that she is hearing Jochen talk about it all. That life before she knew him, which never seemed hidden until now, when so much is being revealed.

— I'm glad she did it, you know. Took us with her.

Bad enough with him as a father-at-a-distance; life would have been intolerable with him as a father-close-up.

— He wasn't interested in us. What we liked doing, what we thought about things. We just didn't exist like that for him.

Jochen's harsh tones are not always easy to bear, but Hannah persists, hoping he might tell her something that will help her understand where this rawness comes from.

— Maybe that's because you didn't live with him?

— No. Ask Karl. He's older, remembers more. No, it was like that even before we left.

That they had no problems leaving the East is final proof for Jochen. Of his father's lack of love. He had his connections, her husband insists; he was not unimportant. Thousands of people put in applications to visit relatives in the West every year, only a fraction were granted. Pensioners were allowed to go: no longer useful, and Jochen thinks they fell into that category. The authorities were paranoid, controlling, but they were not stupid, he says. His mother's application was approved very quickly, although it was obvious to all that she would never return. Hannah stares out at the New York roadscape, listening, not questioning or interjecting, but if she is honest, she finds Jochen's logic a little difficult to follow.

— You always say you're glad to have grown up in the West.

— That's not the point, Hannah. He didn't care. He didn't want us.

It is this aspect that Hannah finds most implausible. After his speech at their wedding, her new father-in-law asked her to dance. Jochen had warned her that he would be difficult, had not told her that he could also be so nice. He spoke with her for a long time about her work, her family, her hopes for the future. Made it clear that he liked her, found her interesting.

— As a person, you know. Not just as his son's wife.

Hannah says that to her husband, watches his reaction in the rearview mirror. The sad eyes, the shrug.

What little she knows of her husband's father is that he is a communist.

— Old. Even when I was young. Fifty when I was born.

Nineteen sixty-five. Hannah counts backward to 1915 and then upward again. Eighteen in 1933. She doesn't ask what happened to him under Hitler, knows only two things: that it was probably bad and that he survived.

— Oh enough now, boring, let's change the subject.

— Christ, J. Why do you always say that? What is that all about?

They used to argue like this a lot, when they first started living together. Whenever they talked about

Germany, which they used to do frequently because re-unification was in all the newspapers and Hannah was interested and often brought it up.

— I mean it's complicated. Not really interesting unless you're German, I guess.

— No. No, that's just it. The conversation will just be getting really interesting, and then you kill it with your lame this-is-getting-boring excuse.

— It's not an excuse.

— Yes it is. It is. You say you can't explain it, but really you mean you don't want to. And because I'm not German and won't understand anyway, it means you don't have to. Period.

And most of the time, Hannah would succeed in making her own period in the argument that way, and what she took to be thoughtful silence would follow. Until the evening Jochen called her bluff.

— I don't want to talk about Nazis with you, Hannah.

He said it calmly, matter-of-fact.

— We talk about Germany. We start with reunification, or with my parents, and within five minutes we're talking about Nazis. I just don't want to do it. Enough.

A direct announcement which had Hannah quickly on the defensive.

— But your father fought against them, didn't he? Isn't that important?

— And now I'm supposed to say no, so you can feel superior?

— You just don't want to see any good in him. You can't bear it that he did something brave and right in his life.

— Hannah, at the risk of sounding patronizing: It is a lot more complicated than that.

Hannah was quiet, then, and Jochen was sorry to have been so blunt. Later he did talk about it with her, briefly. Tried to explain a little of how he felt about the *Nazivergangenheit*, the Nazi past.

— I know: It's part of my father's life, and so it is part of mine too. And of course I know it is important. But you don't know my father and you didn't grow up in Germany, West or East. You don't realize how the past sits on your shoulders there. Old Nazis, victims, the people who fought against them. Buildings, street signs, graffiti, newspaper articles.

He shrugged.

— And my father, that's all he could ever see somehow. He was blind to everything else.

Hannah remembers this conversation now, driving home from their upstate weekend. Loves her husband. Knows how difficult it must have been for him to say this, grateful that he made this effort, but still the memory upsets her. Because she knows he does talk about it sometimes. Not with her, but she has heard him on the phone to his brother and in the kitchen on Karl's last visit. In a German so fast Hannah couldn't follow what Jochen said, but she recognized his tones of anger, shock, sadness. Stood quietly in the hallway listening: excluded.

————

— Your husband is from Germany, isn't he?

The midwife's first question after the twins were born. Under her breath, conspiratorial, and with an understanding nod. What is it about him? Not tall, not blond, hardly any accent to speak of, but still unshakably, unmistakably *deutsch*.

Summer goes by, the twins' third birthday, and though Jochen resists, Hannah is persistent. She would really like to meet her father-in-law again, to know more about him. Jochen is not keen on the idea of visiting his father at first, but over the weeks, he does talk more, even starts to volunteer information.

His father wrote articles and books, on the prewar German communist movement and the postwar division. He was considered something of an authority in East German circles, celebrated for a while in left-leaning West German ones too. Jochen remembers finding his father's name in a book at school once, in a list of prominent anti-Nazis, but still he has no pride in his father's ideals, his achievements. On the rare occasions he speaks about them, he is at best sarcastic, at worst really mean.

— Postwar Germany according to my dad, are you ready? In the East there are the good people, the farmers and workers. In the West, on the other hand, are the capitalists and the old Nazis, who will of course stop at nothing in their quest to corrupt and undermine. And so to keep these fascists and exploiters at bay they, regrettably, had to build a nice big wall.

— Come on. He's an intelligent man. It won't be as simplistic as that.

— Okay, granted, I am being less than generous. But to him the cold war was Western aggression, and everything that happened in the East was somehow a defensive reaction. This is what I hate, you see, this hypocrisy.

— The state was hypocritical, or your father?

— Listen, Hannah: My father fought one repressive regime and then used his credentials to defend another. He was so righteous about the journalists who worked for the Nazis, and then he spent his own career writing lies and excuses.

His books are no longer in print but Hannah does find one of her father-in-law's articles in the microfiche room at the university library. The rhetoric is indeed off-putting, but the photo of the author fascinating. Tight-mouthed, guarded. An expression she recognizes from her husband's face.

Their discussions that autumn are often tense, but they argue less and less, and sometimes when Jochen phones his brother, Hannah notices that he will also talk briefly with his father. And then, just before Christmas, a further health scare helps Hannah win him over. When New Year arrives, they fly with their sons to Germany, because Jochen agrees that it is right for them to see their grandfather. That he should see his grandchildren at least once before he dies. He sends them a letter, the old man, in response to the announcement of their visit. Brief, curt, and in English: Hannah uses it as a page marker in the book she takes onto the plane to read to the twins.

> Since you are coming all this way, it would seem a waste of time to just stay in Frankfurt. I would strongly suggest that we pay a visit to Berlin.

— Out of the question.

Jochen nods at the letter over his complimentary drink.

— Why?

— Karl says Dad's not well enough.

— Did he ask your father?

Jochen shrugs. They lose altitude slowly as they approach Frankfurt, and the twins rub their ears and pull their faces into exaggerated yawns.

— He wants to go. I want to go. You and the boys can stay with your brother. I'll take your dad to Berlin.

— It's a bad idea, Hannah. He's too old, ill. It will be a nightmare.

— How do you know?

Karl picks them up at the airport. Hannah tells him about the letter and he sighs, pushing the luggage trolley ahead of him.

— He's up to something.

Hannah sits in the back again, between her sons, who are restless after the long flight. She tries to find cookies and toys in her bag and still keep an eye on her husband and brother-in-law in the front. Strains to understand what they are saying, becomes aware that she is the only woman in the car, surrounded by two generations of her male relatives: all tired and tense, with their shoulders hunched around their ears.

Her eldest male relative responds to her idea of a hire car and a road trip to Berlin with gruff enthusiasm.

— Very good, yes. I am going to bed now and shall see you in the morning.

The twins sleep in travel cots in the living room, and Karl, Hannah, and Jochen eat together in the small kitchen.

— At least no one will print his stuff now. Even if he could still write.

Karl rolls a cigarette, exchanges a glance with Jochen, and then tells Hannah.

— That was the worst time. After reunification, after the Stasi files were opened.

— He worked for the Stasi?

— Yes he worked for the Stasi, one of their informers. Informal coworkers.

— But he wasn't the only one. Thousands of people did that, didn't they?

— Yes, of course, but does that mean he is not responsible for his actions?

Karl doesn't raise his voice, but his tone has changed. He looks at Jochen, then continues.

— He was against the Nazis, he had suffered for the cause. I think he felt that this absolved him.

Jochen opens another bottle and nods at what his brother says. Hannah sighs at the rhetoric, thinks the sons can be just as dogmatic as their father.

— One of our cousins, Sascha, he wrote some critical essays when he was a student. Critical of the government, and so he was thrown out of university.

— What did he write?

— Oh, unkind things about Honecker: nothing earthshattering. But they had been following Sascha for some time, the Stasi. And then without a degree, you see, his career chances were ruined.

— And that is your father's fault?

— Well, it's not certain, of course, but our father lived with them for a while, in Sascha's last years of school. You never know what piece of information brought him to their attention, do you? Sascha says he read things in his file that only our father would have known.

Hannah can feel Jochen looking at her. She keeps her eyes focused just beyond Karl's shoulder.

— Do you know what he thinks now?

— No, he won't engage with me. That's what pisses me off the most. You just draw this blank with him there. No conversation, just this silence, this massive disappointment. Like we've all been a disappointment to him, the whole world, and we owed it to him to be what he expected of us, because he wanted it so much.

— He's an old man. He was old by the time the wall came down. Maybe it's not fair to expect too much of him?

— Oh, come on!

Jochen has been listening quietly, but is irritated now. He raises his hands in a defeated gesture. Hannah thinks he is about to declare the conversation boring and therefore over.

— Well? You don't like talking about the past with me, do you? Maybe your father is not so different?

Jochen blinks at her.

— There is a difference, Hannah.

— Oh, really?

— Yes, really. He still believes the old lies.

Hannah is unsettled by the Stasi revelations. Awake on the sofa bed next to Jochen, heart pounding. She takes deep breaths, but cannot fill her lungs, regrets the late-night coffee, the evening's red wine. Jochen sleeps on and she is angry. Wonders why he and Karl decided to tell her now: to change her mind about the Berlin visit? She goes over their conversation again, those glances exchanged between the brothers, the tight smiles that appeared at her questions. Hannah lies there and resents them. The way they always insist on complication, the impossibility of explanation. Thinks they enjoy their Germanness and all its secrets, and after that she feels lonely and unkind.

She wakes early, finds her father-in-law already in the kitchen. He smiles and waves a silent good morning. Hannah catches herself watching him as he pours her some tea. Can't help herself: She is intrigued. By this blunt man who can be so gentle, by this horribly compromised idealist. It occurs to her, making toast for them both, that she has tried talking only with the sons, never with the father. In her bag she has a road map of Germany, and one of Berlin. Awake now, despite her bad night, Hannah is determined to take him.

The autobahn is dull and the day chilly and gray, but her father-in-law makes good driving company. He finds a radio station without commercials, tells her the names of the rivers they pass over, breaks a chocolate bar into neat pieces, lays them within easy reach on the dashboard for her.

— Strength for the road ahead.

Countless topics considered, discarded, Hannah talks nonstop about the twins for the first hour or so, and although their grandfather is interested, she is uncomfortable, sure he is aware that this is conversational safe ground. They come to a service station, and he suggests a coffee. He finds them a table by the window, and they smile together about the surly waiter and the plastic plants on the windowsill. Hannah remembers how they danced together at the wedding reception, tells herself to relax in the rest room mirror. Back in the car, she lets him ask her questions: is astonished by what he remembers, details even she had forgotten. That she had broken off her doctoral studies shortly before the wedding: the impossibility of combining work and research, the frustrations with her supervisor. He is sympathetic with her anger now over the cost of child care, over having to stay at home because she cannot earn enough to pay for it.

— Yes. It was much easier in the GDR for women to work than now. Good nurseries, and the state paid for them.

He smiles in the pause this produces.

— Sorry. Not propaganda. It's just one thing we did right, I think. Or at least better.

Coming into Berlin, Hannah notices the weather is changing. The outside temperature reads two below zero and the clouds hang low and heavy over the city. She thinks it might snow and worries about the old man getting cold, fiddles with the dials on the dashboard until the heating system kicks in. The autobahn ends abruptly and they sit at traffic lights, blinking in the dry gusts of warm air from the windscreen. Hannah's feet feel cramped and hot in her winter shoes. She can smell her father-in-law now, too. Wonders how often the home help comes to wash him. Too busy inside his own head to remember: shuffling from one room to another, leaving behind a trail of half-read books and papers.

Inside the city the traffic is stop-start and Hannah struggles with the gearshift and the lane changes. Her father-in-law never learned to drive, he says; navigates badly.

The old man sits up straighter after a while, tells her they have passed into the eastern side of the city. The difference seems very subtle to Hannah: same ugly apartment buildings, same oppressive crush of traffic lanes. There are trams to add to her unease here, and they are stuck behind one for a while, the tires singing strangely on the tracks below them.

Visibly excited, her father-in-law navigates them along one edge of Alexanderplatz before roadwork diverts them up Karl-Marx-Allee. Smiling, shifting in his seat, the old man asks Hannah repeatedly whether she can see the TV tower in her rearview mirror.

— Look. It's an impressive sight, really.

He fidgets, turning to look out the rear windscreen, stiff shoulders straining against the belt.

— They built it to stand right in the sight lines of the avenue. Yes, the angle should be right. Just about. NOW. Now, Mädel! What's wrong with you?

He stares at her.

— Sorry. The hire car. I'm not used to it, think I should concentrate on the road.

He coughs, turns back to look through the front windscreen at the wide, straight avenue, its imposing buildings.

— This was called Stalinallee once. Karl Marx is much better.

He nods. Hannah can see the emphatic movement out of the corner of her eye.

— Uncle Joe. So the Americans called him, yes? American communists. Who, I understand, were banned from working for some time, put in prison.

The old man is looking at her now.

— Yes.

— Is that remembered in America?

Hannah changes down a gear, then up again.

— Yes, I think it is. I believe so.

— Did you learn this at school?

— No. My father told me.

She glances at him. He is listening, watching for her reaction.

— And so your father will tell your boys? Or you will?

The lights are red, she has to stop. Has no excuse not to look at him.

— Yes, I think I will tell them. When they are old enough.

— And now you are thinking McCarthy was nothing compared to what we did here. Yes? And I don't talk to my sons about it, do I?

He is right, or near enough, but Hannah doesn't respond. The lights change and she drives on, disconcerted by her instinct to defend, to find relative levels of wrong.

— Is the hotel far now, do you think?

— I have been taking us on a scenic route. Sorry. I may not see this city again.

— Okay. Yes.

The blue signs of the underground stations go by. And then the old man directs them the wrong way up a one-way street, so Hannah has to take a few quick right and left turns to get them away from the angry drivers and pedestrians. She starts to sweat.

— Sorry. They changed the traffic rules along with everything else, it would seem.

Detached. Dry. Hannah unzips her coat at the next junction, catches sight of the damp patches under her arms. Feels the sweat trickle down her sides and drives and drives and says nothing even though she has a feeling they have been lost for a while because her father-in-law spends too much time looking out the window and not enough time looking at the map.

— Here.

They are at a busy crossroads. Four lanes of traffic, trams, bicycles, an elevated train line, but he makes her pull over.

— Stop, stop. Don't go so far from the corner.

— Is this allowed? I don't think I can park here.

— I won't be long.

She has not pulled up yet and he is already opening the door.

— Wait.

But he doesn't listen. By the time Hannah has straightened up and found the hazard lights, her father-in-law is already striding back down the road to the corner. When she gets to him, he has positioned himself underneath the street sign, and is addressing the people waiting at the pedestrian crossing in a surprisingly loud voice. Most of them cross when the lights change, but a few stay to listen.

Hannah steps forward and takes his arm, but he shakes her off, opens his briefcase, and takes out a long piece of white card, on which is written, in black lettering, *Dimitroff Straße*. Homemade. The pen lines are a little shaky, but the whole thing is quite lovingly done, small brass hooks taped to the back. He holds the sign up so the gathering people can read it.

The afternoon is cold, getting dark already. A small crowd has formed around them now, fifteen or twenty people, and Hannah finds herself absorbed among them. Watching her father-in-law gesturing and shouting: a thin man in a thin coat, strangely fragile. The people around her are talking, some of the voices sharp, but others are light, laughing. A train clatters above on the elevated track, drowning the old man's voice out. He points to the street sign above him. *Danziger Straße*. It has started to snow.

Danzig she knows. Gdansk. Once in Germany, now Poland. But Dimitroff?

A young man has stepped forward out of the crowd. Blue hair and torn trousers, he makes an unlikely partner for Hannah's father-in-law, but they shake hands warmly, and then the young man takes the cardboard strip between his teeth and shins up the signpost. When he hangs the hand-drawn words over the street sign, a few people in the crowd cheer, one or two shout angry words, still others walk away. The blue-haired boy smiles triumphant, embarrassed. He slides down a little, hesitates, unsure whether to jump, and Hannah steps forward to help him.

Six or seven people are left now, out of the original crowd, and the old man stands in the middle of them all with his watery eyes, animated hands, pink in his cheeks from the wind. Hannah wonders whether she should go and claim her father-in-law, but the conversation is intense, involved, and she doesn't know if she can stop it. She offers the boy with the blue hair a handkerchief, asks if he speaks English.

— Dimitroff was a communist, in the Nazi times. Thank you.

He wipes his hands on his saggy trousers first, then on Hannah's handkerchief, smiles.

— This is what it was called before, Dimitroff Strasse, when this was East Berlin.

The snow is settling now, blotting the letters of Dimitroff's name, turning to hissing slush under the passing cars. Voices raised and arms, the small group is oblivious to the dark and weather, debating a history of which Hannah has only the vaguest knowledge. She zips up her coat again and the young man gestures to her father-in-law.

— He is little crazy, maybe, but harmless.

— What are they arguing about? Can you hear them?

— Don't ask me, they're all Ossies.

— You are not from the East?

He shrugs.

— No, I am a student here. From Hamburg. Hey!

Hannah does not see the woman hit her father-in-law. Only the way he holds his hands over his face, beret lying on the wet pavement next to him.

— Hey!

Hannah puts herself in front of the old man, finds herself looking into shocked and furious faces. A second or two later, they are already disappearing, backing off, the woman who slapped her father-in-law moving away last. She is crying.

The old man sits in the passenger seat next to her, breathing, and Hannah tries to drive, but her feet shake on the pedals and her arms feel useless. She turns off the main road, parks on a side street, tries to gather her thoughts, the map, the ballpoint circle that marks the hotel. The boy with the blue hair said it wasn't far, easy from here. She will just stop for a moment, just to calm down a little. The old man sits quietly, blinking, his shoulders curled around him. Hannah rests a hand on his back but he doesn't respond, and after a few minutes she decides to take it away again.

Trams pass, people, the streetlights are on, shop signs: evening. Hannah wonders how she will describe the scene to Jochen. She feels excluded, but also in a way relieved. Not German.

> *(After German reunification, many streets in eastern Berlin were given their pre-GDR names again. One such street was Dimitroff Strasse, which returned to being Danziger Strasse in 1995. Georgi Dimitroff was a communist and one of three men falsely accused by the Nazis of setting the Reichstag fire in 1933. He defended himself in court, humiliating the Nazi lawyers, and eventually winning his case. —R.S.)*

BLUE

The boy arrives early. He is a young man, really; older than he looks. Soft down on his upper lip, no bum on his legs. He has come for the keys, a wad of crumpled notes in his pocket. The neighbor takes him across the landing, keen to get the matter over with. The boy looks the flat over, unhurried, but he's excited about something. It shows in his skin. The flat is a shell with curtains. In the kitchen the cupboards hang off the walls.

— You square with Malky?

The boy nods, the neighbor leaves.

Kenny hadn't planned to stay in the flat until he'd done it up, but now he's here, he doesn't want to leave. He lays his blankets on the floor, takes the curtains off the window, and wraps himself up in a warm corner. Streetlights flood the room, the long, bright shape of the window all along one wall. Kenny lies, eyes wide open in his scratchy cozy curtain nest.

He spends his first two days scrubbing the place down. The kitchen floor makes him retch; the stink of the muck in the corners where the hot soapy water has soaked in. He pours neat bleach in a bucket and sets to work. His fingers itch all night, but the clean floor in the morning inspires him to scrub the walls and the window frames, too. That afternoon he goes round to friends and family for donations. His granny gives him an old washing machine, and he gets a fridge and a cooker cheap from a friend of his brother's.

Kenny's dad brings the whole lot over in a borrowed van, and they haul everything up the stairs together. Between appliances they drink cans of lager in the kitchen and watch telly on the portable that Kenny's mum gave him. Her own one from the kitchen. At midnight, they decide to plumb in the washing machine and give it a trial run with the curtains. Kenny's dad leaves after the cycle finishes, too far gone to drive the van.

The third night Kenny sleeps soundly. The windows are open and his brother's sleeping bag undone, night air on his skin.

In the morning, Kenny climbs up through the attic onto the roof. He spreads his curtains out to dry, half bricks on each corner. He's not too steady on the sloping tiles, but he enjoys the height and the sun. He looks out over the city for a while, tracing the path of the river, identifying landmarks. Kenny's never lived so close to the center before.

— What you doing?

A girl stands by the chimney, same red hair as the neighbor across the hall. The sun is behind her head, so Kenny can't look at her straight.

— What you doing?

— Minding my own.

— What you doing with the curtains?

— Feathering my nest.

— What?

— Never mind.

The girl shifts from one foot to the other, and when Kenny ignores her, she turns on her heel and goes.

Kenny lies back down again, glad to be left alone. He allows himself a midmorning kip to make up for his short night.

A couple of days' work gives him enough money for some paint, a duvet, and a mattress. He finds some chairs to go with the table he hauled out of a skip, and buys some pots and pans with his giro. Kenny has enough stuff in the flat now to live quite comfortably. Part of him misses the emptiness, the adventure of making do, but he doesn't think Maria would like it. He needs some rugs for the floor. He has been here for two weeks.

He calls her from the phone box on the corner, but she knows already. Someone told someone, who told someone else, who told her sister, who told her yesterday. Maria is difficult to talk to this evening and Kenny can't think straight. He can hear her sipping her tea, tapping her rings on the mug, and his money is running out. He invites her round, giving her directions over the pips. Kenny hangs up and can't remember if she said she was coming or not.

The bulb in the bathroom has gone, so he has his bath in the dark. He can hear the people downstairs arguing, even when he puts his head underwater. They keep going until his bath gets cold. He puts the fire on when he gets into bed, and wakes up in the night with a dry mouth and gummy eyes. The people downstairs are shouting again, but Kenny drops off before they finish their row.

The day is endless. Kenny has the TV on for company. He buys some food to cook for tea and a bottle of wine, but then he remembers that Maria might not want to drink, so he goes out again and buys some orange, just in case, and some candles, which he fixes into a clean ashtray. He sits on the bed for a long time and then goes out to buy a newspaper, but he can't concentrate. He smokes too much, and opens all the windows to get rid of the smell. He tries to have an afternoon nap, but watches TV instead. He doesn't want to cook until she comes, but he's starving. He runs out to the shops to get some crisps. The light is going out of the day, and when he is back in the flat again, Kenny worries that Maria has come and gone while he was out.

When the buzzer goes he doesn't get up immediately. He stands next to the entry phone and counts to ten, and then he answers.

— It's me.

— Okay.

Maria takes a while to get up the stairs. When she gets to the second floor, Kenny can watch her over the banis-

ter. He hasn't seen her for over a month and she's showing now. Skinny woman with a big belly. She is walking
like his sister did when she was pregnant, only her back
is still straight and her legs look good. She pauses on the
landing and looks up.

— Do you want a hand?

— I'm okay.

When she gets to the top floor, she stands in front of
him for a couple of seconds to get her breath, and he
doesn't know what to do.

— Can I come in, then?

Kenny is proud of the flat, clean and bright with its
improvised furniture. He shows her everything, linger-
ing in the kitchen with its washing machine, hurrying
through the bedroom with its double bed. Maria is quiet,
nodding, noncommittal. Kenny wants her to smile at him
and say nice things, like it's good to have a gas cooker.

— I'm starving.

He gets her a cup of tea and a biscuit to tide her over,
and she sits in the kitchen while he cooks. He asks after
her family and she smiles while she answers, but she's not
being friendly. There are long silences between them,
and Kenny tries to look busy with the food. He sets the
table and she sits with her hands folded on her belly.
Then he opens the wine but says she can have orange if
she wants, and she says a glass of water will do.

— I didn't ask you to do any of this, you know?

— No, I know.

This throws him a bit, but Maria is more relaxed now and they eat. Kenny has some wine and feels a bit better.

— I wanted to do it.

Maria nods but she looks out the window. He thinks she might be laughing at him, but the moment passes. He spoons the peaches out of the can into bowls and they both help themselves to ice cream. She has a sip or two of his wine without asking, and then she picks up the peach tin from the side and spoons more ice cream into the left-over syrup and eats it from the can, leaning back in her chair. She tells him about work and friends, and he tells her about family, and neither of them mentions the flat or the baby.

Maria says she wants to watch TV, but when she sees that there is only the double bed to sit on, she changes her mind. They stand in the narrow hallway, both embarrassed, and then Maria says she wants to go home.

Kenny helps her into the cab. Maria looks like a kid on the backseat. A kid with a pillow stuffed up her jumper. She smiles at him and then she's off.

Kenny lies in the bath and can't cry. He brings the candles into the bathroom, dripping water through the flat. He drinks the rest of the wine, rolls a damp joint that is a job to smoke but is just the trick, and he can forget it all until the morning.

It's Sunday and he goes to his mum's for dinner. He eats a lot and helps his dad wash up, then he falls asleep on the sofa watching the sport. His mum asks if he wants to stay over, but he's too old to be sleeping in bunk beds so he goes back to the flat. He buys lagers on the way and drinks a skinful so he can forget it all for a little bit longer.

Kenny spends a day in bed. He goes to sign on. He does a day's work for his brother-in-law, who gives him a sofa and some paint. He repaints all the doors in the flat, and starts on the skirting boards. Then he phones Maria.

She sounds happy to hear from him and they chat for a while about this and that. She tells him her dad's got work again and he says that's really good news because it's been about three years hasn't it, and she says, over. Kenny can hear that Maria is smiling while she talks about how happy her mum is and how everything will be easier now. It makes him smile too and forget to listen properly, and so he nearly misses it when Maria says she'd like to come over tomorrow evening. He says fine, and then they say good-bye and Kenny's back in the flat before he knows it. He sits in the kitchen and stares at the TV.

It's late when he wakes up. He has a bath and cleans the windows. He doesn't want to sit around waiting like the last time, so goes for a walk in a park, which is something he would never normally do. Then he gets a bus across the center of the city, sitting on the top deck. On the way back, he gets off at the river and walks across one of the bridges. It's late afternoon when he gets to the other side and he realizes he has no money left to buy anything for dinner. He gets a bus to his mum's to borrow a tenner till he gets his giro. She's hurt because he's in a hurry, so he promises to come for Sunday lunch.

When he gets back, Maria is sitting on the step outside the block, but she's not annoyed. Tells him she was early, thought she'd wait a bit. She looks relieved.

They cook dinner together and eat in the kitchen, not saying very much, but feeling quite cozy. It gets dark and they wash up together, and then Maria says she would really like some chocolate.

She is lying on the bed when he comes back from the shop. He throws the sweets on the mattress and sits down next to her. She has a sip of his lager and eats her chocolates and they watch a film together and she falls asleep. He stares at her belly and her breasts and her legs for a long time and then he covers her up and goes to sleep on the sofa. He hears her get up and go to the toilet, but she doesn't come into the living room, so he doesn't go back into the bedroom.

She stays for breakfast and helps him finish the skirting boards, but after lunch she goes home. Kenny washes up and then he has a bath and he thinks about Maria. About all the times they slept together before, and how he doesn't know if sleeping together now would be a good idea or not, but he wants to all the same and he hopes she does, too. He's already been in the flat for a month.

It's Saturday and he's got no money, so he spends the day in bed half watching telly, mostly thinking about

Maria. He needs to pay the rent soon. He needs some money for food and fags and bus fares. When the baby comes he'll need ten times more. He does some maths on the back of an envelope and it all adds up to needing a job. Sunday lunch tomorrow: He'll ask his brother-in-law.

His brother-in-law says he'll ask his boss, but he can't promise anything. His sister tells him to look in the paper like everyone else and his dad tells her to be quiet. She is for a minute or two and they all eat, but then she says that Kenny shouldn't have got Maria pregnant in the first place if he doesn't have a job, and Kenny's dad swears at her. Kenny's mum leaves the room and then Kenny's dad gets angry and Kenny's brother-in-law just carries on eating and Kenny thinks that would be me if I was married to Maria and sitting in a family row. He has to pay the rent, and he owes his mum a tenner, and he knows she worries, and he has to chew every mouthful twenty times to distract himself from throwing the dishes around the room. Sprouts in the shag pile, gravy on the walls.

Kenny's dad comes round and takes him in to work. Only there's nothing for him to do and Kenny thinks his dad is probably paying him out of his own pocket, which is like taking five tenners off his mum and giving her one back. After the second day he tells his dad he's got some other work. Kenny's dad knows he's lying, and Kenny knows that he knows.

He goes to sign on. Pays the rent, gives his dad a tenner for his mum, gets a bag of fifties for the meter, and buys a week's worth of bread and beans. He gets a paper every morning and takes a pile of coins to the phone box to call for jobs, but there's nothing doing. It rains a fair bit that week and Kenny wishes he had a phone so Maria could call and it wouldn't be up to him to swallow his lump of pride every time. He holds out over the weekend, and then on Sunday night the buzzer goes.

Kenny goes down this time and keeps Maria company up the stairs. She's a bit bigger again and she looks good, even in the damp stairwell.

They settle down on the bed quite quickly and turn the TV on but leave the light off. The room gets darker and they get under the duvet, where it is warm, and Kenny feels Maria's legs next to his, her belly pressed against his ribs. They share a can of lager and stay like that until it gets late and they're both sleepy. Maria slips to the edge of the mattress and takes off her trousers and socks. She leaves her knickers on but takes off her bra under her T-shirt. Then she gets back under the duvet. Kenny kicks off his jeans and turns the telly off. The room is quiet and dark and neither of them moves for a while. Kenny really needs to pee now, but maybe Maria will fall asleep while he's out of the room. He puts a hand on her arm. She breathes steadily and doesn't move. Kenny gets up quietly and goes to the bathroom.

He pees in the dark and brushes his teeth and decides to talk to her in the morning.

Maria rolls over when he gets under the duvet and puts a hand on his stomach. He touches her fingers and then strokes her arm, and then he rolls over and strokes her back. He can't see her in the dark, but he knows her eyes are open. He kisses her and she puts her hands on his chest. Kenny takes his T-shirt off and then he takes hers off, too. She is uncomfortable, but he thinks she's beautiful.

He isn't sleepy. He wonders if it was the right thing to do. She doesn't say anything, but lies very still next to him. After a while, she rolls onto her side and goes to sleep. A little later, she rolls over again, putting her back to him. After that, Kenny goes to sleep, too.

In the morning he cooks breakfast and they eat in bed. Kenny reads the paper while Maria has a bath. His brother comes round with the paint and an eighth. They whisper in the narrow hall so Maria won't hear. Kenny's brother smiles, pats him on the elbow, and says he'll leave them to it.

Maria gets back into bed to read the paper and Kenny makes a start on the bathroom. She comes in after a while with a cup of tea for him and he asks her if she likes the color. She nods, but doesn't look too certain, so Kenny says she can choose the color for the big room if she likes. Maria shrugs.

— Blue.

— If it's a boy.

— Yeah. Whatever.

She comes back in a bit later with her coat on. The paint smell is making her a bit sick, thought she'd go for a walk, buy a pint of milk.

Kenny waits.

He doesn't turn the lights on when it gets dark and he doesn't cook himself any dinner, he just lies in the bed. He can't cry and he can't sleep. He lies very still and smokes his brother's eighth.

At the end of the week Kenny cashes his giro and paints the living room blue.

He goes to the phone box and calls his brother to see if he can stay over. He rings his mum and says he won't come for Sunday lunch, but he'll see her soon. Early evening, Kenny hands the keys back to the neighbor and walks out of the estate onto the main road.

ARCHITECT

The architect was young and enthusiastic, energetic and ambitious. He had a quiet passion for space, for dimensions, for awe. For comfort, for splendor, and for ease. This passion was undimmed by the pragmatics of fire escapes, minimum sanitation requirements, cost-effective building materials, and optimum car parking arrangements.

The architect's designs were singular. His drawings and his gracious manner somehow inseparable. Bureaucrats with construction millions would comb their hair and run a checking tongue across their dentures in preparation for their meetings. Those clients who fell for his designs invariably also fell for him.

Small articles had begun to appear in specialist journals, respectful in their appraisal. The architect was treading a unique path and considered himself a lucky man: Success and all its grand gestures, though still distant, seemed inevitable.

Today, however, is different.

All week the architect has struggled and strained, but what he has produced bears no relation to his expectations, and he feels critical of every line he has drawn. Although he can name each fault, he cannot make improvements.

It has never happened before and he is determined not to let it worry him.

Another project requires his attention. A simple matter of redrawing the car park. Twelve executive spaces are required, not ten. He allows this task to stretch over three working days. A minor incident on the face of it, but his boss is puzzled. Upset, even, though he does not show it. The partners discuss the architect over pub lunches and the secretaries start sugaring his coffee in sympathy, falling silent when he walks by.

The architect tells himself it's nothing, that he just needs a break. He rings his brother and goes for the weekend. They are drunk, they are sober. They talk women, politics, work out an old grievance, and resolve again to visit their father more often. Each feels happy with the time spent together.

The weeks go by, as they do, and the architect keeps busy. Long hours with little time for brooding, reflecting. Returning home from a conference, he reads his first newspaper in days. A new public building on the front page. Half the world throws hands up in horror, the other half claps hands in praise, and the architect skims the articles, avoiding the fact that he has no opinion.

Evening falls and he allows himself another look at the newspaper. The building is a puzzle to him, a shape. He cannot assess scale, proportion, quality. His mind's eye sees no interior. A cold cloud gathers in his belly. He cooks dinner and watches TV.

At work, two glaring errors in a recent front elevation have been noted. The boss wants a word. The architect retires to the associates' washroom to think matters through. That elevation was done before. Before what? Before.

He starts crossing the road to avoid construction sites. He takes unpaid leave. On the telephone he tells friends that he is pursuing his own interests. He learns of others' successes and tastes his first bitterness. He wants to confess. If I could laugh about this with someone. But he is ashamed of his feelings and buries them deep, where they hurt most.

The days fall by, all swift and all exactly the same. He can no longer read newspapers, much less journals. Television is distressing rather than distracting. His savings are dwindling and the mortgage is a worry. He considers other careers. Each seems attractive for a day or so, an hour or two, but nothing lasts. At night he dreams structures, wakes hopeful, and forgets them.

He asks his father for a loan, and it turns into a row.

— I'd like to see what you're designing.

— You wouldn't understand it anyway.

— If your mother were alive.

— If you were the last person on earth.

The dismissal notice from his boss—brimful of disappointment and regret—rests behind the clock on the mantel. Barely read, unacknowledged. It didn't happen. He never had that job.

The architect spends as much time as possible outside, driving out to the country at dawn, and only returning after dark. He turns no lights on in the house, and fantasizes about being found dead on a hillside. Flat on his back, arms outstretched against the damp ground. He imagines the last thing he'd see would be sky, blinkered by the long green grasses fluttering against his cold pink cheeks.

He talks to no one and worries about the need to be something worthwhile, meaningful, substantial, good. He worries about being boring.

His brother is impatient, irritated. Why doesn't he get some work, stop sponging off Dad, think about other people for a change, get on with it? The architect sells his house, his car, his record collection, and moves in with his father. Back in his old room with the Meccano under the bed, the architect feels much better.

His days are spent sleeping and eating. His dad takes him to the allotment and sets him to digging so his boy will get some movement. He discusses sowing patterns with his son, and weeding strategies. Frosts and pests, composts and companion plants. And though the architect is quiet, his father is glad to have him around because he loves him very much.

His brother comes to visit regularly, and even brings his girlfriend once. She has a thoughtful manner and lovely hair. His dad is happier than he's been in weeks, cracks jokes and opens an extra bottle.

After dinner, she washes while the architect dries, and he asks her to take off her clothes. She is charming, unfailingly polite, and ignores his request. The rest of the evening passes without incident, but his brother comes round the next morning with harsh words. On the way to the doctor's, his dad tells the architect that he really mustn't say such things. At lunchtime, his father's eyes are red, but he heats the soup as usual, and they even listen to some music together.

Three months later the medication is reduced, although the twice-weekly hour of silence with a counselor continues. The architect doesn't tell her that he no longer has ideas. That floor plans make his chest ache. That he dreams of staircases crumbling beneath his feet. He knows all these things himself, and he also knows how banal they are. Instead he cries a little, and after she expresses approval, he cries a great deal.

He starts looking in the paper for jobs. Wills himself to search through the architectural appointments, but finds his mind stubbornly closed to the idea. The shame of this is almost too much to bear, and he is regularly nasty to his father. Both know this is uncalled for, neither says anything about it.

In job interviews he cites an elderly parent as a reason for leaving his last employment. A change of direction was needed, he smiles, confesses. Dad was the catalyst, really. The old charm trickles back again from the brink, and the managers understand crossroads, family commitments, appreciate the honesty, the evidence of storms weathered. Not all of them think this makes him employable, but he soon has a job.

A month in, over dinner, he tells his father and brother about it. That he is enjoying his new work and feels relevant too, in an engaging but not too demanding way. Dad is pleased. It is exactly the life he wanted for his boy. But his brother is angry. What has this whole bloody crisis been about? They argue in hissed whispers in the kitchen, so their father can't hear. A glass is smashed to diffuse the tension. His brother is ashamed, sweeps up the glass, and leaves.

The architect rents a flat nearer the office and starts sleeping with the girl who lives downstairs. He visits his brother to patch things up, and soon they are making up a foursome at weekends.

Sometime later, he realizes he has been walking in and out of buildings without thinking about them.

He visits his dad regularly, too, and they often spend their Sundays working together on the allotment. On one such visit, his father expresses concern about his tomatoes. They are suffering from the unseasonal cold, and urgently need protection.

The architect looks around at the other allotments and is shocked and amazed by the ugly ingenuity of crooked panes and corrugated iron. Sodden, splintered window frames forming crude but effective structures. Plants thriving below warm condensation.

He gathers materials from the tip, from skips, from the waste ground by the canal. Dad potters happily, tying up the runner beans, only half aware of his son, who sits in the doorway of the shed with a brown paper bag and pencil, and sketches a rough idea in the early afternoon sun. By evening, a splendid construction surrounds the tomatoes, complete with a hinged door for ease of picking.

Dad is overjoyed. Son is proud and pleased and also sad. The sun still shines, but the wind has picked up, and the rawness of a day spent outside is in his face and fingers.

The doubt that came from nowhere and disappeared again without reason. The turmoil and confusion, concession and healing. The arguments, bitterness, and lessons learned. All these have left the mark of compromise on him. He is stable and disappointed. No longer an architect.

THE LATE SPRING

Be careful, then, and be gentle about death.
For it is hard to die, it is difficult to go through
The door, even when it opens.
—D. H. LAWRENCE, "ALL SOULS' DAY"

S pring was late in coming: The bees needed feeding. The beekeeper was walking with honey pots in his pockets. One mile north along the line of the valley, up on the rise above the stream. The hives seemed farther from the house this year, and the old man kept what felt like a steady pace, but his progress through the winter grass was slow. Eyes set on the first group of beeches where his hives were placed, he had been thinking about the neat row of cones for days: backs to the east wind and the sheltering copse, westward faces watching for the spring bloom of the blackberries, the wildflowers' first flush. Waiting. The beekeeper's legs were a year older again, and his heart, and he stopped often on the narrow path. Standing, breathing among the wet clumps of grass. And this is when he saw it.

A speck of movement, easier to see out of the corner of one eye. A small shadow, beating a steady path across the low plain below him. Upright, not animal. The old man stopped, held in his rattling breath. Stood watching the dark fleck and its dogged progress. No one else lived at this end of the valley, only him.

The beekeeper was transfixed by this small, human disturbance in the flat land. Had not seen a soul since winter began, perhaps longer. His eyes brushed the valley for other movements, company for the speck: a hunting party, perhaps, or woodcutters if the village stocks were low after the long cold. But the rolling copse and grass were empty as always. The common lands of the nearest village were just visible from where the beekeeper was standing: Half a morning away for a young man, and the villagers rarely came beyond them.

As the speck came closer, the beekeeper could see how it faltered, as if searching or undecided, and he wondered if it might be afraid: strayed too far from home, seeking familiar ground now, the assurance of the track to the village. The old man could just make out the sunken line of it to the north; the muddy cut in the sodden valley, which healed a half mile after it left the commons, overgrown with bramble and grass.

Below the beekeeper, the stream ran deep and close to the foot of the slope, and here the speck wavered, stopped. The old man crouched low in the grass at the top of the rise. Aware for the first time he too might be observed, if the figure chose to cast its eyes upward. They were no more than sixty paces apart now: close enough for the old man to see it was a child. A spare little body, with long hair to its shoulders. Small chest rising, falling, face turning first upstream, then down. The beekeeper watched the slight figure hesitate on the shallow bank, listened to the high flow of water against rock. He thought, *turn north;* if it walked north along the stream it would come first to the mossy bridge and after that the track. But the child did not turn, slid instead down the bank, gripping briefly onto rock, then letting itself drop into the fast water.

The old man stood up sharply, out of the cover of the grasses. Watched in dismay as the child slipped under the surface, out of sight: The day was gray-cold, with an east wind and the water melt from the mountains. When, a few seconds later, a few yards downstream, the child's fists broke the water and then its face, the old man recoiled. But instead of the drowning, or indeed lifeless, form he expected, the small figure stood up in the icy black flow, found its feet, and started wading.

The beekeeper's first thought had been to help the child, but second thoughts came now, with fear not far behind. It unnerved him, the small form, in its obstinacy, wading on. Arms high, chest deep, stiff-necked: willful. Even at this distance, he could hear the child's breath, coming in gasps: a sharp noise which tugged at the old man's insides, had him flinching, withdrawing into the trees. Fingertips reaching for bark, seeking cover of the bare winter branches, the beekeeper kept his eyes on the child as it clambered, dripping, out onto the near bank. Its clothes clung dark-wet to its narrow frame, and it stood a moment, sodden, shaking. Then, on limbs fine as spindles, it stumbled, gathering itself again: walking, soon quickening, making ground, leaving the flat run of the valley behind. The old man watched, heart uneven, as the child moved faster, leaning into the slope, grabbing at handfuls of the long grass, pulling itself in a true line up the hill, toward the beeches where the beekeeper was standing.

Seen. The old man shrank back farther into trunk and twig. Retreating, fleeing to where the trees grew thickest. *Just a child, just a child, but what can it want from me?* He cowered, breath too fast and loud. Came to feed his bees, and now he hid himself. Tight bundle of elbow, knee, and rib; eyes down, fixed on the mossy ground. Listening.

Time passed, breath slowed. No sound came, save the familiar valley noises of wind and water. The old man waited a few minutes longer and then uncurled, slowly, as his stiff limbs allowed, standing gradually straighter. He was careful to stay within the cover of the beeches, moving cautiously to where he could see out through the branches, survey the hillside, the valley again.

Old eyes watery, he blinked, searching out the fine movements of the child among the grass and shrub. But there was no trace of it: on the slope, the track, in the bushes, by the stream. It had disappeared.

The heavy grass was lank, bleached pale by the winter, the trees on the horizon stood black and wet and bare.

The winter had been long and the hive stores were low. The old man mixed honey with water from the stream: a full pot for each cone, for his bees to feed on. He checked the walls for tears and gaps, mending with plugs of moss and wax. Palms resting gently on the woven surface, he pressed an ear to each of his hives in turn. The bees had retreated deep into the comb, but the beekeeper could hear their wings. A warming hum under the wind in the beeches that still showed no green.

Late morning and clouds gathered on a cold wind. There were other hives to check over the next rise, but the old man smelled ice on the air and turned for home. Slower than he used to be, afraid the weather would be faster than him now. Frost racing him back along the valley floor, gripping already at his fingers, its cold ache crawling into the joints.

Snow fell in the afternoon and the beekeeper took up his winter place beside the fire again. The day was dark beyond the door, the snow thick and gray. He could barely see where the treeline started, when afternoon ended and evening began.

———

A life spent with bees and eating honey. Toothless since middle age. Gruel with honey, hot water with honey, spoonfuls of honey in the morning. The beekeeper had seen times of plenty: used to trade with the villagers, back when his hives dotted the valley. Now he kept them only as far as he could walk, trusted in his bees to provide for him. Not reliant on anybody. Kept a few chickens, and they laid their eggs for him in predictable places. Sowed summer and winter vegetables, barley, gathered what he didn't grow from the valley. Elderberries, wild garlic, nuts, and mushrooms.

The old man had his father's eyes and bones, hips which jutted like a woman's, large kneecaps, and long thighs. Long gone, the beekeeper rarely thought of him now; his mother remembered only as a tight grip above the elbow. No brothers, no sisters, no neighbors; silence came an age ago and never left, the years going by unnoticed. Color bleeding from his hair and eyes, unheeded; flesh falling into soft folds under the hard line of his chin. He shaved, and where the skin hung loose, the bristle grew feathery white, undisturbed by the razor.

Bees were the rhythm of his year; blooms and birdsong marked the turn of the seasons. Fifty harvests he had seen, perhaps more, *no matter:* He lived in the certainty of another, his life an unfailing cycle of spring summer autumn winter spring. Until this year, when a child came instead of the expected mild winds.

————

The beekeeper sat by his fire but could not settle. Remembered the child dropping into the stream, and then afterward, how fast it moved, seeming to come up the rise directly for him. His four walls around him, fingers itching in the warmth of the fire, he doubted now that the child had seen him at all. *Fool.* Still, as he turned the day over, the old man could feel his heart again: the sudden fear up on the slope, as though the small figure had come for him; and then the relief later, when it was gone again. He shifted until he was comfortable on the straw and sacking. Not cold, but aware of the winter in his bones. He imagined the snow covering the long grass of the valley now, the spare trail of broken stems left on the slope by the child. The beekeeper closed his eyes.

In the beeches again, but not hiding this time: searching quietly through the trees. He finds the child sleeping and he is not afraid. A still figure, lying in front of the hives. Snow blows in across the clearing, a smooth drift forming against its curved spine.

When the old man woke it was night and the house was cold. Outside in the woodpile, he found first an old shawl and then a small, taut body beneath it, curled against the logs. Cold to the touch, but dry and still breathing. A boy. He carried him inside.

————

Careful not to warm him too quickly, the old man let the boy sleep. Young and slight, he was no weight at all to carry and seemed even smaller lying there in the corner by the fire.

The child's few clothes, soaked from the stream, were rigid in the chill night, stiff as dry leather, and the skin beneath was blue, joints chapped and weeping. It seemed impossible, but the boy was still alive, pulse low but regular, pumping visible at wrist and ear. The old man wrapped the naked limbs in rags, covered them with straw. He fetched more firewood, and then snow to melt for cooking. Bitter outside, but his lungs felt tight in the smoky room and he didn't like to be too close to the low shape curled in the corner.

While he worked, the beekeeper tried to remember the villagers who had bought his wax and honey. Families, two or three generations he had known. They had come out to him in their carts, on foot, each autumn. With cloth and fat for trading, sacks of wheat, baskets of apples. The boy might be a grandson or great-grandson, but his narrow features called no faces from the old man's memory.

What he does recall are whispered exchanges, inquisitive glances: whole families come out from the village to look at the bee man. Children watching from behind their parents' legs, running if he came near them. Women talking to him, smiling, but their eyes always sharp, always moving, surveying his small home and its smoke-blackened contents. He knew they liked his honey, and the trade was good, but he hated the staring and the questions, which got worse as he got older. Didn't know why he should feel lonely, why it should be safer in the village. Always lived here, always would, and he couldn't understand these people, why they chose to spend their days all stuffed together, but could never find a way to tell them.

The slight figure was touched gray by the shadows beyond the fire, and thoughts of the villagers made the old man uneasy: He had never been afraid of bees but sometimes of people. Always glad when the honey was sold again, the season colder, his solitude returned.

A day passed, the snow stayed, the night was cold and wakeful. The boy lay by the embers, the beekeeper sat against the wall, under the blanket, folded over, doubled up against the winter that wouldn't end.

The child woke briefly on the third morning, when the sky was clear, and the old man stirred an egg into the boy's soup, spoke to him for the first time.

— Too much snow to go home now. Too far from the village. You can wait here.

His voice a cracked whisper, barely audible. The child blinked and ate and then slept again. The old man kept the fire stoked and fed the boy each time he woke, but when, on the fourth day, the child was running a fever, the old man decided he should find the boy's family. Brave the cold and the village.

———

The snow was knee deep around the house, but thinner on the path by the stream. The day was bright and the bee-keeper kept to the flat ground, took the long way round to the old bridge and the track that led to the village. It was dull cold under the blue shadow of the poplars, and the old man walked carefully with two sticks but still fell. Feet sliding on rocks hidden by the snow, knees giving way beneath him.

His hands were raw, legs and trousers torn, when he got to the track. The old man breathed a minute or two, bent forward, leaning on his sticks, and when he raised his head to start walking again, he saw he was not alone.

Men up ahead, two of them, with an ox and cart, laden with wood for burning. One wheel was caught in the frozen, rutted track and their voices were loud, words blurted like curses. The beekeeper raised a stick, waving it in the bright air to draw their attention, and when the tall man at the ox's head held an arm up in greeting, he started on his limping journey toward them.

The second man came round the back of the cart, watching him.

— The bee man.

— Come through the winter, then.

The cold air was still and clear and the beekeeper could hear their conversation, the note of surprise at his survival, could feel the weight of their curious eyes on him. Wishing to make the encounter as brief as possible, he started to explain, calling before he got to them.

— I have the missing child. In my house.

The men looked at him. His voice was hoarse, it caught in his throat. He thought they mustn't have heard him.

— The boy.

The words scratched at the cold air and the men said nothing. He stopped, still a couple of paces away from them.

— He is small and his hair is long. Came the same day as the snow and he is sick now. Should go back to his people.

The old man shifted his bony feet, could feel the icy track through the soles of his boots. The sun was bright and the two men had their hands raised, shielding their eyes.

— There is no boy missing from the village.

— Are you sure he is one of ours?

— He's in my house. I found him.

— But he is not from the village. We have no child missing.

The tall man repeated himself, face drawn into a brief frown, like a question. The other man laughed.

— You found him, he's yours, I say. We've more than enough already.

The beekeeper looked at him, wanted him to come and

take the child away but couldn't find the words to tell him. *Not one of theirs.* He waited, but the tall man didn't speak again: He patted his ox, took hold of its head to guide it, and the laughing man turned away, too. Steadied the load as the cart lurched over the rut and on. Nodded farewell, rolling away from the beekeeper, back toward the village.

— Where do you come from?

The sky was darkening when the old man returned, and the boy awake under the straw.

— You are not from the village. Where do you come from?

But the child did not answer: only closed his eyes again.

The day turned to quiet, moonless dark, and the bee-keeper coaxed the fire back to life. Washed the cuts on his legs first and bound them, then cooked up a pot of gruel; enough for two and some left over for the morning. When he looked up, the child was standing. Arm wrapped tight around his rags, eyes fixed hard on the door, he seemed to be listening.

— What is it?

The old man took the pot off the fire and waited. It came again, the wail and yell, outside, somewhere deep in the center of the valley. The old man whispered:

— Fox.

And then:

— Sounds human, yes?

The boy looked at him, gray eyes unblinking, and the beekeeper was not sure that he understood him. The fox cried again, and the old man pulled on boots, a blanket over his shoulders, went out into the cold. Beside the house, the coop door lay slanted: the fowl inside easy prey for a hungry fox in a winter-bound valley. The old man righted the panel, fixing it firmly, scolding himself for his carelessness: It should be he, not the boy, who was watchful.

The child was lying by the fire again when he came back in. The old man stirred the embers to warm him, took a fistful of dried berries from the jar by the far wall: something sweet, a small reward for the boy to chew on. He heard the fox a few more times as he cooked and again later while they were eating. The beekeeper watched, but the boy did not look up from his food, and the noise retreated back farther into the valley.

The light died off slowly from the fire, the fox was gone, and the old man was aware of the wide emptiness around his house, and of not being alone. He lay down for the first time since the boy came, on his own straw bed, on the other side of the embers. Still uncertain of being too close to the child, but the comfort of company was unexpected, soothing.

A memory came, unbidden, before he slept: of the spring when his father had stung him. He couldn't say now how old he was then: just about the same size, perhaps, as the boy in the straw before him.

After the frosts had gone, his father carried a small handful of bees back to the house each morning, and his mother stood him at the door to watch his father coming. For weeks they followed the same routine: his bare arm gripped by mother's hands, bee pinched tight by father's fingers and pressed against his skin. Mother let him cry, father waited, then scratched the sting out of the blister with the long curl of his thumbnail. The burning welts on his arm, the hot sickness that came with them, closing down fast on eyes and throat; the same the next day, and on those that followed. Until the blisters stopped coming, and there was no pain any longer, no nausea, and he pulled the full comb from the hives for the first time that autumn.

The old man lay on the edge of dreams, planning. His father had more than doubled his stocks back then, and now he could do the same. Breed new queens, build more hives: It would be hard, but four hands could do five times the work of two; he had learned that from his father. The winter had been fierce, too long, and so perhaps he had been right, the laughing villager: The boy had come to him, his now, a gift from the valley.

But in the morning, the boy's fever had returned, his sick breath coming fast and shallow. Afraid, the old man sweetened cool water with honey, lifted the boy's head, fed him in spoonfuls. He could see the small throat leap with each mouthful: restless eyes under blue lids, shuddering heart inside the narrow chest.

The beekeeper cursed his idle dreams; the child was sick, not apprentice, or heir; he didn't belong here. Still pale as the winter grass and he still smelled cold, like wind and river. The old man had been caring, feeding, and warming for days now, but the boy was getting no better. His eyes were dull, his limbs weak, and he cried while he was sleeping.

The beekeeper went over and over the events of the first morning: He had a dying child on his hands, could allow himself no more illusions. The boy came from the direction of the western slopes. The old man had never been beyond the valley, but he reasoned to himself that the boy's people must live there, over the far rise, perhaps a whole village. Where there is one child there is usually another, and with them come fathers and mothers. They might be looking for him now, or gave him up for lost when the snow came.

There was gray light under the door, wind coming through the cracks in the wood, but it was not cold. Outside, the thaw had started, water dripping from the eaves as the day gathered. The old man boiled eggs for the child in case of hunger, told the sleeping form he would be back with help as soon as he was able. His people, beyond the western slopes, they would not know to come here and get their boy. It would be quicker if he went to them.

The far hills were still snowbound but the valley was softening. The old man walked north along the stream, which sang with new water from the thaw. His legs were bound tight with rags, and the going was easier than the last time; the snow not so deep now, patches of brownish grass and earth colored the low banks. Soon he could see the mossy bridge, still frosted white, and the straggly copse, somewhere beyond which lay the common lands, the village. Late morning, he began to cut across country, retracing the boy's steps across the floor of the valley.

In his mind's eye a journey, a lifetime ago, with his father. A warm day, early autumn, and a runner had come panting to fetch the bee man to the village. Had taken them out to the orchard where a swarm had descended, so heavy it had bent the branches of the fruit trees. The beekeeper remembered leaves brushing the grass below, and the almighty, ten-thousand-fold hum, mesmerizing, thrilling. Women and children locked in the houses, men with tight faces watching from behind the orchard wall, keeping their distance. His father, tall, a shadow over his long features, laid a wide strip of linen in the grass, and then waited. The bees crawled along the white cloth, covering it slowly with their thick, black bristling. Teeming to the empty hive, which was lying open and ready, walls smeared with honey.

His father had taken the money: He had been paid handsomely, but he did not seem pleased. They did not carry the hive up to the beeches as he had expected, did not take the new colony and set it up beside the others. Instead they drove the cart away from the village along the stream, stopping at the place where the rocky banks leveled off, and the flow was deep.

He did as he was told, stayed alone in the cart, watching. While his father took the full hive, the bees trapped inside, and held them under the water.

Shaken by the memory, the old man stood still. He had started up the slow rise of the western slopes, but could not walk again for a good few minutes. Only when he realized how late it had become did he force himself on again. There was no sun visible to judge time by, but it was certainly well after noon: the light weaker than before, the day less convincing. The slope was steep, hurt the old man's lungs. He stopped more often, tried to keep his breathing even, but still to keep going. Could see the last swell of ground now, which would take him out of the valley. His fingers were dead-white, gripped around his sticks, and he didn't like to look at them. Nor at the clouds over the brow of the hill, heavy with rain to come.

He hoped the boy's village would be close. That they might feed him there, drive him home, or offer a bed to rest on.

No trees at the top, no shelter, but then nothing to obscure his view, either. He looked for plumes of smoke from stoves and chimneys, or for low clumps of houses, strips of cultivated land, for walls and fences. The sky was gray and low over the unfamiliar country, rolling on for days in all directions. The old man stood and held in his rasping breath, watching for signs of life in the land ahead.

Wind, treetops, water, clouds. No human movement or human sound.

The rain came, swallowed the land, the old man. He was not strong now, let it take hold of him. Was aware, after some time, of having left the bone-jarring slope behind, of being back on the flat plain of the valley. He did not look for a marker to fix his course, but kept his head down, face out of the pelting rain, eyes almost closed.

His thoughts circled, uncontrolled: the empty land beyond the valley, the child in his house that had come from nowhere. Could no longer picture the boy's face, his form, only grass and rain: had sought him out and now he was gone from him again.

The storm was above, but the old man's sticks found the ground ahead and he did not falter. He felt little in these hours, not cold or wet, nor pain or hunger. He saw the bees held under by his father's hands, spoke a few words aloud as he stumbled.

— Old stock. Too late in the season. They would have died anyway: too weak to suffer the winter.

Soon the light would fail and he was too slow now to make it home before nightfall. He thought of his own bees, under the beeches, waiting for the warmer weather. Then of the dream he had, the day the boy came: no fear, just a slight figure on the ground in front of the hives, sleeping. The rain let up, and he could see the first low rise ahead, the familiar trees on the gray horizon.

The day was almost gone when he reached the clearing. There was no snow by the hives, the ground was dry, and while the wind touched the tops of the trees, below them it was still. Just warm enough for his bees to be flying.

The old man watched the small bodies navigate the outside air, listened to the strange barking sound of his breath. He filled his lungs, but his heart could not find its familiar rhythm. He moved in closer to the hives, standing between them, letting their comforting hum surround him.

No blossom yet, but his bees were busy, bringing out their winter dead. Small carcasses on the dark earth before the hives. He laid himself down beside them.

THE CROSSING

He has been there since dawn; head down, keeping pace with them.

Marta can see for miles along the broad riverbank, and she has kept one eye on his progress all morning, urging her children on, hoping they haven't seen him. Marta is frightened. They were making headway till they hit the river. Every hour's delay brings danger closer. *And now the man.* She has been walking her family along the wide surge of water since late yesterday afternoon. The anger from the east at their backs, she has kept them moving, one eye behind her, the other on the thick swirls of current churning the water slowly over and under.

Pressing on, praying for a way across, Marta carries her baby at her chest and a bundle tied to her back. Her eldest child, a daughter, walks in front of her with their bag, and her young twin boys walk behind. The river defenses have been damaged in the fighting and Marta can hear the boys' boots squelch in the marshy ground, tramping in step with one another, in step with her. The grass is long, the going uneven: They walk as if they are wading already. Moving on in silence, below the line of

111

the flood barrier, level with the water, parallel with safety on the other side.

She looks back at the man and he is still there: no closer, no farther away, but with his head up now. Watching. White smudge of face under a black hat.

Marta drops her pace momentarily, ushers her sons past her, putting herself between her children and the stranger. If she keeps pushing, Marta thinks, they can stay ahead of him for another hour, maybe two. *He will give up. Drop back. There will be a way across the water.*

Up ahead she sees a bridge. The tall pillars are still upright in the slow current, but nothing connects them: bombed, and the remains washed away. Marta helps her children up onto the road that rises steeply to the bridge. She reasons with herself, fights down the disappointment. *There must be another, farther along there will be another.*

— We'll keep going.

The twins run up the slope and stand at the edge where the road stops and twisted fingers of metal poke out of the blasted concrete. They lie on their stomachs, heads dangling over the edge, calling down to the water. Their laughter throws echoes around the tall columns, and Marta is afraid the man can hear them. They have slowed down: He could be in earshot now. Doesn't want to draw any attention to them, not out here where there is no one to help them and no way of knowing what might happen. She walks with Ani, her daughter, holding the baby close, calling to her sons.

— We're not stopping.

But now Ani isn't moving. She is pointing and pulling at her mother's arm.

— There's a man.

Marta knows he has gained on them, before she has even looked round. Less than one hundred meters now, still walking, looking straight ahead, breaking into a run. Marta can see the mud on his trouser cuffs. Yellow on black wool.

The twins run down to their mother, oblivious to the man, who is almost at the bridge now, white wrists reaching long and thin from his black sleeves. He is speaking, but Marta can't hear what he's saying. *He should be shouting if he wants us to hear.*

The twins are excited; they rush at their mother.

— We could swim it, Mama.

— It's not very deep.

Marta pulls them sharply off the road, eyes fixed on the stranger, walking her family away from him, daughter behind her, arms around her boys. She wants to turn, but there is only the rise of the road between them, and she can hear what he says now.

— It's not deep. I've done it.

But Marta doesn't hear the words, only the accent, beating pulse in her throat.

— I've been across here before.

The familiar rhythm. *One of us.* The relief makes Marta shake.

The stranger stops on the road. Still talking, still breath-less. His neck is long and thin, and his head is bony. Full of black teeth, white gums. A hard mouth but a voice like home.

— It's a good place to swim.

The stranger looks at Marta, smiles, and nods. His eyes are dark. Friendly. His voice is right, but still she keeps away. He wears boots bound in rags, and Marta can smell him, his sour breath and skin.

— We'll walk on.

She gathers her children again, urging them farther down the slope along the riverbank, away from the bro-ken pillars, the road, the man.

— We'll find the next bridge.

Marta's palms are pressed flat against the backs of her twins, pushing, her legs straining under the weight of the baby, the days spent walking, the bundle on her back.

— They bombed all the bridges.

The voice is polite, still breathless, but gentle. Like the eyes. The man stays where he is at the water's edge, stand-ing, watching the departing family. Marta looks round at him, and he smiles, then squats down and puts his hands in the water. Marta pushes her children on.

— The river turns farther up. You'll be walking east again soon.

Marta stops. Her heart turns over. Her daughter has hold of her arm.

— I don't want to swim, Mama.

The twins push at her sides, two sets of eyes fixed on the man at the shore.

— It's not deep. Tell her, Mama.

— We saw the bottom.

— Mama, no.

Marta knows he is watching her, but the stranger keeps quiet, and keeps his distance. She crouches down, shifting the weight of the bundle across her back. She lifts her baby boy, holds him tighter, full of misgiving. The river is wide. Thirty meters, maybe more.

— I can help you. I swam across before.

Marta waits one minute, two, and when he doesn't move she shrugs the bundle higher onto her shoulders, walks down to the water, keeping a few meters between herself and the man.

— Mama.

— I know, Ani.

She can see the bottom, but it is chest deep. Over head height for the twins. She looks over at the remains of the bridge. Each of the pillars has a wide base, a shelf just below the surface. The stranger points.

— We can swim between the pillars, rest on the shelves.

— It's too deep.

— We'll take it in stages.

Ani calls to her mother from where she stands with her brothers.

— I don't want to, Mama.

— Only four meters between the pillars.

— Quiet, Betim.

— Only four meters, easy.

— Leka, I said be quiet.

Marta turns back to the stranger, shakes her head.

— Our things will get wet.

— It's hot. You can dry them, camp for the night.

— The bags are too heavy.

Marta walks back to her children, lifts the bundle onto her back again. The stranger runs along the bank, gathering driftwood. The boys join in.

— Only the big bits, boys. Bigger, twice the size.

Marta watches.

— What about a boat?

— I've been walking the river for days. No boats.

Ani kicks the ground next to her mother. Marta looks on as the man gathers driftwood with her sons.

— How will I get the baby across?

— Tie him to me. I'll swim with him.

— No.

The stranger ties the wood together into a frame. A handkerchief at one corner, his shirt at another. Betim offers his vest for the third and Leka ties off the last corner with a sock. The stranger carries the frame down to the water. The bag sags through the middle, heavier on one side than the other, but it floats.

— I can pull it, see? I'll take this over first, come back for the bundle.

Marta doesn't look at him. She can see the road snaking off into the distance on the other side of the river; can feel the breeze on her face, blowing from the east.

— It will take half an hour, an hour at most. You can dry your things. Walk on in the evening.

Marta picks at the knot holding the bundle to her back.

— It's safe over there. You can rest, stop for the night.

— I'll take the baby, not you.

— Very good.

The stranger takes off his boots and ties the laces together, draping them around his neck. He wades out into the water until he is waist deep and starts swimming, pulling the bag after him. When he gets to the first pillar he waves. Water streams out of his sleeve in an arc, and the twins both laugh and wave back. They run to the water's edge, but Marta stops them.

— Yes, wait. I'll come back and help you.

The man gestures them away, then turns and swims to the next pillar. The boys crouch, watching, tying their laces together as the stranger had done. Marta squeezes her daughter's hand and tells her to take her boots off.

The stranger is past the middle of the river now. Still swimming. He hasn't looked round again, and Marta wonders absently if he will come back and help them. She calculates what is in the bag. *Food and clothes.* The last tins of meat. But no money, no valuables. *No great loss.* The stranger wades out onto the far shore, pulling the raft behind him. He doesn't look round or wave. He walks up onto the road, out of sight. The twins both stand up and turn to look at Marta. She shrugs, makes a mental list. *Three tins, the half loaf, the blankets, one coat.* She still has the oilskins, the twins' jackets, her wedding ring. *No food.*

The stranger walks back off the road into the river. He doesn't have the bag with him, and his jacket is tied around his waist. His chest is bright white against the brown riverbank. He waves and starts swimming again, only stopping at the middle pillar on the way back. He speaks to them as he swims, even before he is in earshot, skin glowing through the water, shoulder blades working like sharp wings.

— There's a good spot for a fire, and I've spread the blankets on bushes to dry.

He is out of breath, greenish. He crouches down on the bank, breathing hard, the twins standing next to him, boots dangling ready around their necks. Marta takes the thinnest blanket and tears it in two. She holds her baby's back against her chest and tells Ani to tie the blanket round both of them. She sees the stranger stand up out the corner of her eye.

— You should tie him to your back, then he'll be out of the water when you swim.

— I'll swim on my back.

She knots the other half of the blanket firmly around herself, angry. The baby's arms are trapped under the blanket and he struggles as they walk down to the bank.

The twins set the bundle in the middle of the frame, and the stranger tells them to wade first, then swim. He says he will help Marta, but Marta says he should help Ani instead.

The twins wade out, holding the bundle at waist height, then swim, steady and serious, aiming for the first pillar. Marta watches them drift out in the current, shifting their course, kicking hard, her heart hammering in her throat. When they get to the pillar, Leka climbs up onto the shelf and waves. Marta waves back and the stranger turns to her.

— Strong swimmers. Good boys.

She watches her twins set off for the next pillar, small bodies working hard against the wide water, tells herself: *They are strong swimmers, good boys.*

Ani allows the stranger to take her hand, and he leads her into the water. She looks round at her mother, but carries on walking until she is waist deep.

— It's cold, Mama.

— But you are brave.

Ani slides into the water and swims, shouting and splashing, but Marta is not so afraid this time. The stranger swims beside her daughter, and when Ani waves from the first pillar, Marta can see she is smiling.

The twins are still swimming on, over halfway there. She can see their shoulders, hunched round their ears with the cold, but they keep going, jumping back into the water from the pillars, pulling the bundle between them, ever closer to the safer shore. Marta ties her boots around her waist and wades into the river. The stranger helps Ani up onto the shelf by the second pillar and treads water.

— Go back! Wait. I'll come for you.

Marta ignores him and carries on wading. Her baby shifts against her stomach, uncomfortable in his blanket binding. He tries to look up at her face, breathing fast, soft head pressing against her chin. Marta has her arms around him, frightened to let go, although he is bound tight to her chest. The riverbed changes from sharp pebbles to soft mud, silky against her feet and warm compared to the water. Marta sinks up to her ankles in the slime, and the water reaches her thighs.

It is much colder now she is out of the shallows. Her ankle bones ache and her stomach contracts, shrinking back from the water. The slow pull of current bends her knees. Her baby's feet skim the water and he shouts and kicks, bright splashes of cold in the sun. Marta knows the stranger is swimming toward them, shouting at her to go back to the shore. She turns her back to him and lies down into the water, keeping her arms wrapped around her baby, kicking her legs.

The cold knocks the air out of her lungs. Her boots fill with water, drag down at her waist. She puts her arms out to keep herself afloat, but too late, and she pulls her baby down into the river with her.

When they surface, he is screaming rigid against her chest, arms straining to get out of the blankets. Marta has the gritty river taste in her mouth. She can't feel the bottom, toes reaching, legs straining, kicking. Her baby's head is underwater again. She thrashes, pushes her arms out to steady herself, coughing, arching her back. She hears her baby's screams through a wall of water, like ice around her neck. Her boots kick heavy at her thighs as she fights the current. The baby's head is out of the water, but his body is in the cold river with hers. Water floods Marta's mouth. She sinks again.

The stranger swims underneath them, his arms under Marta's shoulders, pulling her chest up out of the water and the baby with it. Marta retches, wants to cry. The stranger pulls them onto the pillar, swiftly, steadily, murmuring, breathing, kicking beneath them. He pushes Marta up onto the ledge, jarring her cold bones against the stones. She stands up out of the water on weak legs and the stranger unties the blankets. He is not angry, which surprises her. The baby still screams, but with tears now, and not so stiff. Once his arms are free he pulls himself up against his mother and presses his face into her neck. Ani is standing and watching at the next pillar, arms wrapped round the stone; the twins are watching from the opposite shore. The stranger shouts to them to build a fire, and tells Ani to wait until they get to her. She nods, silent and shivering.

The baby screams when he is pulled away from Marta's chest, fists and feet attacking the air in fury. The stranger lays him quickly down again, high up against Marta's shoulder blades, and the baby wraps his arms round her neck. The man reties the blankets around the baby and around Marta's chest. He pulls them tight and the baby cries, but Marta makes no protest. After he has checked the knots, the stranger slides back down into the river. He holds out his hand, bare arm reaching out of the water.

— Ready? Come on.

Marta stops. Eyes fixed on the reaching arm, her heart working, painful. The stranger's words resound in her ears: same voice, different rhythm. Same language, different accent. But familiar, too.

The beat of fear in her chest. The shouting outside her house. The rhythm of the day the men were taken away.

Marta looks at the stranger and he meets her gaze. Eyes dark, lips moving.

— Come on.

No pretense now. *One of them.* The stranger has a stranger's voice. As if the river has cleaned his throat, icy water washing the lie from his tongue.

He takes Marta's hand and she sits obediently down on the ledge, slides into the water. Her children are up ahead, she can't go back, she has to go on. The baby grips her neck, but he is quiet now. Marta swims with the stranger to the next pillar and he smiles encouragement, swimming alongside her on his back. Ani helps her mother up onto the ledge and they rest in silence while the stranger treads water. They swim on together. When they get to the last pillar, they wave to Leka, who is waiting for them on the shore.

— We've built a fire!

He gestures over the rise, where Betim stands, eating a chunk of bread. The baby starts to cry again as they wade out of the water, but he is not angry anymore, just cold. Ani's lips are ringed blue and Marta can't feel the stones under her feet. None of them can undo the knots in the baby's blankets; even Leka's hands are still weak with the cold. Marta turns to the stranger for help, but he is back in the water, jacket on again, swimming away, already beyond the first pillar.

Betim calls from the rise and waves, but the stranger doesn't look round. Just swims on in silence to the eastern shore.

DOG-LEG LANE

The family—the boy, his mother and father—have lived on the lane since shortly before he was born, and he knows no other home. Three now, he can talk. And walk with his mother to the shops at one end of the street, his nursery school at the other. If they go to the playground or the market, then he still gets wheeled in the pushchair. The lane makes a dogleg turn at the far end into a cul-de-sac, where the slides and swings and the weekly veg stalls are found. Not far from the flat—the parents-to-be were happy about that when they moved here—but still too far for a just-turned three-year-old's legs to carry him there and back. He sleeps in the pushchair on the way home. Dozing lips parted, head swaying over to one side. And when his mother reaches to straighten his neck, he wakes slightly, rustle of carrier bag in his ears, blue-white, red-white plastic stripes framing the view from the corners of his half-closed eyes. Stuffed with tomatoes sweet potatoes leeks bananas and slung over the pushchair handlebars for the rolling journey home.

His mother tells him:

— We're very lucky.

Nursery school, shops, doctor's surgery, library.

— Everything we need, it's all here.

And when his father comes back from work and lifts him up to their second-storey window, the boy can just about see it all, too.

— Promotion!

His father stands in the hallway with flowers. Home early, very happy, he smiles and tells his boy this is really good news.

— Shall we go out? Clare? Have a meal.

His mother pulls the largest bloom from the bunch and sticks it behind her ear. Laughs.

— What do you think?

They go out all together for the first time ever and eat in the Indian across the road. The sun is setting, the streetlights are lit, and the way home takes only three minutes, the boy between his parents, feet on the tarmac, arms stretched high and wide. One hand held by mother, the other by father, they swing him high over the single yellow line, the gray curbstone, the cracks and sweet wrappers of the pavement, to their front door.

Perhaps they tell their son that night, that they will be moving. Perhaps in the restaurant, or maybe one evening in the week which follows. Over a dinnertime or bath time, or on one of those mornings when he gets up early and climbs into their bed. An unremarkable moment which passes without incident, a small part of a larger routine.

Every new job, every couple of years or so, it's just what they do. Eleven years together and five homes, Dog-Leg Lane by far the longest lived. The promotion is to a different branch, and has immediate effect. The other side of the city, a long train ride away, and unless they move, the boy will hardly see his father. Besides, the schools are better, there is less traffic and litter, more green space.

Coming home from the nursery at lunchtime, the boy's mother decides to take her son to the top floor. Their building has six storeys. Hardly a tower block, but still she remembers the upper-landing window being high enough to look out over the rooftops facing east. They went up there, she and her husband, when the council offered them the flat. It was a sunny day, clear sky, and they looked good: the red roof tiles against the blue.

— It's a surprise for you, sweetheart.

She wants to show her son the place where they will move.

The stairwell has been cleaned in the morning. Smells of disinfectant and of lunches being cooked. She makes a game out of climbing, racing her son up each flight and letting him win. They look out on the third floor, but the view is not so different from their own downstairs. On the fourth floor, she says:

— Look, we can see the next street from here.

— But not ours.

And her son presses his cheek to the window, trying to look down, but the angle is too steep.

On the fifth floor, the boy doesn't want to play race games anymore, so his mother gets to the sixth floor first. She can see farther than she remembered: over to the hospital chimney and mosque, along the dark brown run of the railway tracks which her husband now travels. She holds her son up at the window, points, and describes. His eyes follow her fingers and lips and she enjoys the touch of his breath on her face, his weight in her arms.

— You see?

And he nods and they stand with their foreheads and fingertips pressed to the glass. It is not so blue today, the tiles not so red. But still, she thinks. It's still a nice view.

— Pretty, don't you think?

— No. I don't like it.

The boy shakes his head.

His mother looks again for something nice out there to show him, but her son pushes against her arms and she has to put him down.

———

She is sad, of course, that her son didn't like his surprise, but she knows him, and that like all children, he has his tired days, his moods. She thinks he might be coming down with something: He doesn't eat much dinner that evening, and then he cries in his bath.

Over breakfast the talk is of council swaps, housing associations, and new nursery schools. The boy watches his parents and pushes the banana slices around on his toast. His mother says:

— Come on, sweetheart. Eat your breakfast, please.

But he doesn't, and now she is only half listening to her husband, mostly watching her son.

— Do you want some honey maybe? On your banana?

The boy shrugs, and his father is watching them both now, wife and boy.

— Or peanut butter?

— Clare?

— Yes, sorry. I am listening. I just don't think he's well.

— I should get going anyway.

— Peanut butter.

The boy pulls his plate along the table with him, leans against his mother while she spreads peanut butter on his toast, mashes the banana into it, and then spoons honey over the top. His father has shoes and jacket on now.

— We'll talk about it tonight, then?

— Yes, promise. Tonight.

They smile, kiss good-bye, two, three times, and the boy climbs between them into his mother's lap. Mouth

full of banana honey peanut butter toast breakfast, his
face and voice sticky.

— I don't want to move house.

They have a morning routine. Watch Dad going to work
from the second-floor window. After breakfast and before
teeth brushing, mother and son. He always stops at the
dogleg corner and waves back in their direction before he
makes the turn. He can't see them, of course, not from
that distance, and the angle is all wrong. But he knows
they watch him, and likes the fact that they do this, so he
always does his wave, every day.

That morning, though, the boy eats his breakfast very
slowly. And when his mother holds out her hand to take
him into the living room, he ignores her. She stands and
watches him chewing for a minute or so, then decides not
to force the issue and loads the washing machine instead.

So when her husband gets to the dogleg corner, he
waves and smiles at nobody before he makes his way
across the playground down the alley to the station and
then work.

They are on waiting lists now and get brochures in the
post. New housing estates near train links, good primary
schools. The boy's mother empties the letter box each
morning when she takes her son to nursery. She doesn't

go straight home, but takes the fat envelopes to the café down the road. Her daily treat. Milky coffee and some dreams of what could be. Soon.

Ballpoint crosses near her favorites, she takes the marked brochures home and spreads the city map out on the living room floor. The maisonette with garden is near a school and a park. Two hospitals in the area, so she could work again. Agency nursing perhaps, and then a regular day shift, when the boy starts school.

After lunch, after his nap, she lies down on the bed by her son.

— What shall we do this afternoon?

— Swings.

She smiles.

— I've found a new park with swings and a pond. Do you want to see on the map?

She carries his sleep-warm body into the living room and shows him the lines which represent their street and all the other roads around it in the center of the city. Spidery black outlines, filled in pale yellow, pink, and green. She takes his hand and traces the run of the lane, guiding his finger along and round the dogleg. And then their hands hover together above the main arterial road into the city, and she says:

— We could even get a train to the new park today. Or a number seventy-three. All the way. Look.

She begins the wide arc with their arms, from the lane

out to the suburb where the maisonette lies, but her son shouts and snatches his hand away.

— No!

He holds his fingers in a fist close to his chest, then wedges them under his armpit.

— It was weird, Mark.

Her husband shaves in the evenings now, to save time in the mornings. She sits on the edge of the bath and watches him.

— Like I hurt him or something, but I was just holding his hand.

— He'll get used to it, love. He's three. Two weeks in the new place and he won't even remember Dog-Leg Lane.

— I suppose so.

— I know so. We'll go to this place together Saturday, he'll see the garden and the park, and it will be fine.

But on Saturday the boy refuses to get dressed. And when his mother says they will take him to the new flat in his pajamas, he screams until he can't catch his breath. They decide to try again after lunch, call the housing association. Only the boy makes his same shrill protest in the afternoon and on Sunday morning again.

— Next weekend, then.

But the next weekend the boy is ill. Just a cold, but it drags on for over a week in which none of them sleep properly and the new brochures pile up, their envelopes unopened, the contents unread.

Day off work, wedding anniversary. They both take their son to the nursery and then go back to bed. Late morning, and husband and wife walk down the lane together, holding hands. She buys wine and olives, he chooses a ripe mango treat for their son. When they pick him up at midday, the other parents smile congratulations: Their boy told the teacher, has made them a card.

Evening, bottle open on the kitchen table, and son asleep in bed. The parents sit up late, their talk of past and future, the kitchen light off, hall light on, lips and teeth tinged dark by the wine.

— We should maybe give it another go, what do you think?

They look again through the housing brochures, their son's glue and tissue-paper card.

— Will you talk to him, love?

— I'll talk to him.

And they smile at each other, at each other's wine-stained smiles.

But their son frowns and kicks at the chair legs when his mother talks to him. Puts his hands over his ears. And when she shows him the pictures in the brochures, he punches them away, neck jutting forward, hands in tight fists.

— What is wrong with you?

———

The father does well in his new job. A pay rise already, only two months in. They have more money, fewer debts, but less time to spend together. The trains are slow, and if the boy's father doesn't make his connection, he doesn't get home until after his son has gone to bed. He misses him.

They get up earlier to compensate: Breakfast is now their family time, mother and son in pajamas, father fully dressed. It is getting to be winter, so it is dark outside while they make their toast and tea, and it is a tired and silent meal.

Standing at the window, watching her husband walk to the corner, the boy's mother whispers to her son:

— It would be so much nicer for Daddy. For all of us. If we lived somewhere a little closer. Don't you think?

And the instant she says it, she feels the change in his breathing, his body tightening in her arms.

She puts him down, crouches next to him.

— What is it, love? Please tell me.

But he won't look at her. Face set, knees locked, fingers like claws.

His mother doesn't tell her husband; she makes an appointment and takes their son to the surgery.

— It's not normal. I mean it just doesn't feel like normal behavior.

The doctor listens absently, watches the boy watching his mother.

— All children have times when they feel insecure.

His mother is angry, but also embarrassed. Perhaps it is nothing to be worried about after all. She calls a friend who says my god yes it's been ages hasn't it, and of course you can come over.

So she puts her son into his pushchair after lunch and walks him through the market to the swings. But when they get past the playground he starts crying, and at the mouth of the alley his tears turn to low screams. His mother stops.

— No, please.

But the pitch goes up, and her son twists his body, straining against the straps. His small face contorted, white. His mouth red and loud. She pulls him out of the pushchair and holds him.

— Please, sweetheart. Stop.

His body is hard against hers, limbs unbending. She can feel his heart. See the mothers on the playground looking at them, the people in the market. Standing by the alleyway with her boy who won't stop screaming in her arms.

— It's like he's afraid of something.

— In the alley?

The boy is in bed. His mother has called her friend, apologized, and now she phones her husband at work.

— It was that same screaming again.

— But maybe it's about something else now.

— No. I don't know. Can't you just come home? Please?

They argue and she hangs up. Stands at the living room window, closes the curtains against their second-storey dogleg view.

— What is it, sweetheart? Can't you tell me? Nothing will happen to you. I'll be with you and it will be fine.

But it is the same every time now. Whenever she tries to go beyond the lane, he cries. She reads books, calls family, friends, help lines for advice. If they walk, his limbs become rigid. In the pushchair he throws his weight from side to side. She tries reason, bribery, authority, pleading. They battle, mother and son, and he always wins. She can't bear his stiff body when she carries him. Can't put him through it. Is afraid of the screams.

Her husband listens to her crying when she phones. In the evening, she shows him the marks left by their son's fingers on her arms.

— He wouldn't turn the corner with me. I couldn't make him. He was doing that. He was holding my arms like that, see?

He watches his son sleeping, then picks him up, carries him into their bedroom, and the parents lie down in the streetlight dark with their boy between them.

— You could get your old job back. I'm sure they would give it to you.

— I thought of that, Clare. I thought it, too. But it's not a solution.

— No, not long term. But maybe he just needs another six months or something. If we just told him we'd be staying, then maybe he'd be all right.

— We don't know that, love. Do we?

She doesn't say anything, knows he is right. It wouldn't be a solution, either, it would just be lying.

The boy is thin, so is his mother. They have had concerned looks from the other parents, gentle questions from the nursery teacher.

— You know. Anything we can do.

She tells her husband.

— I could have cried. I said thank you.

They go back to the doctor, together this time, and she listens more attentively, looks at the bruises, the rings under their eyes.

— I have a colleague who can perhaps help you.

She writes the phone number down, the address. They leave it one more week, still hoping for a change, and then they phone him. His practice is on the outskirts of the city.

Her husband borrows a car from a colleague. A child seat from another. He straps it in to the back, and his wife watches him from their second-floor window. The way he stands by the parked car a moment, murmuring, lips moving. The frown lines cut into his forehead.

They drive along the street away from the dogleg dead end. The boy's mother in front with her husband at the wheel, son in the back, high and upright in the bright padding of the child seat. He can see out all the windows and she worries, wonders whether they shouldn't shield off at least some of the view. Midday traffic, red lights, red buses, and roadwork. They make their way slowly through the city streets and his mother watches for a reaction, a flicker. He moves his lips gently, but her son seems calm.

She turns forward, checks where they are, looks at the map. Whispers to her husband.

— Third left.

And her husband says:

— He's got his eyes shut. His eyes are shut, love.

He is looking in the rearview mirror. She looks round at her son. A minute ago his eyes were open and he was looking, but now he is pale and his eyes are firmly closed.

She looks at her husband. He has slowed to a crawl, head bent low over the steering wheel. She thinks he might cry.

— Park the car.

— There's nowhere here to park it.

— Park the car.

— We're on a red route, Clare. Illegal. We can't.

The cars beep behind them. Drivers hanging on to their horns. The streets running off to the left are blocked by concrete bollards. A high metal barricade runs along the center of the road to their right. The boy sits silent in the back of the car, face ashen, fingers and feet trembling. His father swears and his mother takes off her safety belt, turns, and touches him, his cold hands and legs. His eyes dance under his eyelids, but he does not respond. She pulls herself up and over the seat, and her husband drives on. The people in the cars beep and overtake. They drive slowly past them in the fast lane, watching the mother make her clumsy way into the backseat to be with her panic-stricken son.

She pulls off his straps, her boy into her lap, holds his head under her chin, small body in her arms, and sits. Eyes closed in sympathy.

Her husband watches them in the rearview mirror, watches the road ahead for a place to turn.

Christmas comes, and they make their excuses. Don't invite family, don't invite friends, decline invitations. The holidays fall between weekends that year, and so the father is home for twelve full days.

It is claustrophobic at first, just the three of them. In the flat, mostly, but they also go to the café when it's open, and when it's not raining, the swings. And then they get used to this. Talking about nothing much. Cooking, eating, walking, swinging, sleeping, sitting. Heating turned up, carols on the radio, toys on the floor, condensation on the kitchen window.

The lane is quieter than usual. Families away, shops and restaurants closed even after Boxing Day. They walk past the tinsel window displays together, boy between his parents, hand in hand in hand. On the wet pavement dotted with chewing gum and across the empty marketplace with its cigarette butts and puddles. The weather turns cold and they wear heavy coats, scarves, hats, feel the grip of each other's fingers through layers of mitten and glove.

They wake together in the mornings, the three of them, lie blinking at each other. Too warm under the duvet, but none of them thinking about getting up.

Sometime around New Year they run out of bread and milk. Think the shop by the swings might be open, but when they get round the dogleg they see that the shutters are down.

— What about the one opposite the station? Just at the end of the alley.

— You stay with him, then? Play on the swings with Daddy, sweetheart, I'll be back in a sec.

His father swings the boy high, but he is watching his mother walk down the alley. Only one eye showing, face turned into his anorak hood.

— She'll be back before you know it.

His dad catches the swing, and the boy slides off, runs to the start of the alley, and stops. His mother has turned the corner, out of sight. He turns back to his father.

— She's fine. She's just gone into the shop.

The boy turns away again. Takes two, three steps into the alley, and his father stands ready. Waiting for him to stop and scream, but he doesn't, he just keeps slowly walking. And when his mother comes back round the corner with the bag of bread and milk, he is already halfway down the alley. She stops still, is silent for a moment, and then says:

— Hello, you.

The parents see each other from opposite ends of the alley. White faces above dark coats, under hats.

Their son has stopped walking now. He looks from mother to father, one to the other, looks frightened, and they both walk toward him, slowly, trying not to run.

They cook dinner and eat together, go to bed. The winter day behind them like a small, unexpected gift.

Their son was trembling as they carried him home.

They both felt his breathing fast and high, saw the skin around his eyes, blue-white.

But no one asked, or begged or forced him.

The boy sleeps and his parents lie in the dark, afraid to talk, even to think about it. Frightened, grateful, awake.

FRANCIS JOHN JONES, 1924–

*"My life before I came into the army was uneventful but
full of childish dreams."*

PRIVATE H, 1944 (in *A War of Nerves* by Dr. Ben Shephard)

The story he is going to tell happened in 1944.
— Not a story.

Fran corrects himself. Sitting by the window, looking
out of it mostly, rather than at me. Says he'll tell me about
an incident in the summer of that year, the way he sees
it. Knows I have heard something of what happened already: a family secret, discussed in loud whispers. A stigma
for his daughter: Other dads had medals. Less so for her
sons: the safer distance of another generation. I work
with one of them, and he asked about my Ph.D. in a lunch
break awhile back, making conversation, said I might find
his granddad interesting. Probably thought I would never
take him up on it, and I wonder now whether Fran took a
lot of persuading. I expected reluctance, belligerence even,
but I don't know how to describe him. Gentle handshake,
biscuits and tea laid out on the table.

Fran should have turned twenty in Italy, with his battalion, only he got sick and spent his birthday outside Cairo. In the army hospital, with the wounded, the amputees. Heat like he'd never known: days spent dozing, staring at the ceiling fan. Nights wakeful, listening to the other men dream.

— Frightening sometimes, that noise. Especially when I had the fever.

Jaundice followed. The medical officer said six more weeks. He would join his battalion late. Further up the line. Couldn't be helped.

His eyeballs were still yellow when he got to them. Inspected in the small square of shaving mirror that first morning: He could only see fragments of face. Pink forehead, tight with sunburn; sickly tinge of eye laced with fine red veins; upper lip soft with down. He soaped his cheeks, got his razor out.

— Bloody hell, Jones, is it worth the effort?

Thorn was the only man there he knew already. Not well: They had got the same transport out of Naples in February. Never spoke much, never had much to say to each other, but it helped to have someone there he recognized. Always unfamiliar faces, new recruits, battalions fused to make up numbers. People came, then they were gone again.

Fran was the last to join his new platoon. Spent the first day struggling to remember names while they called him Titch because he was tall, and Bones because it rhymed with his surname, and you could still see his ribs, despite the pounds he'd gained those last weeks laid up in hospital.

— Fuck's sake. Look what they've sent us.

This is how Fran remembers his first encounter with Butler, who was joking, of course.

— After a fashion.

There was always plenty of that kind of thing; you came to expect it. Humor in the war, Fran says, was quick and cold. Still, there was a difference to it that summer, in that platoon, something he never got the measure of. The men were not unfriendly with each other, but he never felt they got along.

Fran looks at me a moment, I don't know why. His fingers move, self-conscious, find his tie, smooth it against his chest. We smile at each other, briefly, and I wonder if it was put on especially for the occasion.

The Leicesters had taken the woods at the southern end of a ridgeway, and Fran's battalion was sent up the line to relieve them. Over half the men had gone ahead already, and the remaining platoons, Fran's included, were to march north in the morning. These were their orders, swiftly supplemented by a rumor: Tanks were just a day behind them, on their way from the coast as backup.

— They wanted us to break the line, we thought.

All geared up for something. Sicily, Naples, Rome: forcing the Germans north to the border.

Hot, late summer. They came through villages where people lived in rubble. The country between them was mostly empty, only a few farmers still trying to save some of the harvest. The soldiers stripped tomatoes off the vines as they passed. Crossed a field full of melons, big as footballs, heavy as heads. Still moving, they scooped the seed out with their hands and threw it into the undergrowth. Fran remembers passing stringy gobs of it, moons of yellow-green skin gnawed clean, discarded in the dust. The juice got everywhere, gummed his fingers together, his eyelids, mixed with the sweat on his cheeks and neck. Couldn't escape the sweet stink of it.

At night they heard shelling, but Fran could see nothing in the surrounding dark. They marched on in silent single file, each holding the bayonet scabbard of the man in front.

— I had Thorn ahead of me. But I don't remember thinking about that at the time, mind.

That is what memory does; it organizes. Fran lifts a warning finger. Sifts and turns the events over, he says, and it is extraordinary: how he finds them everywhere now, Thorn and Butler, in all the little details.

Fran knew the names in his platoon by then, and that he was the youngest. One or two had been fighting since the beginning, including Butler, but not their platoon commander. Ash had only six months on Fran, and though he never gave his age, Fran remembers Butler ran a book on it, and most men laid odds that he wasn't too much older.

— Twenty-two, I would say, and in charge of men like Thorn. Twice his age, easy.

The Leicesters had camped in a wood, by a clearing. Tall silver-brown trunks, the afternoon air among them thick and hot. Fran's battalion was bigger, bivouacs spread far back into the trees. Sun getting low when they arrived.

— First walking, then waiting.

Thorn brewed tea for them and Butler slept. Curled on his side, eyes hidden in the crook of his elbow. All around him, other men were doing the same, and Fran was tired, too. Pain in his legs and his back, from the marching, the heavy pack. The tea was sweet, clumped with milk powder, and he was glad of the sugar; still felt the weeks of his illness. He remembers lying down, his limbs sore and heavy, but his eyes stayed open.

Beyond the trees lay the ridgeway. They were to take it south to north, with the tanks behind them. At the top of the first rise was a village, capturing it their first objective. Two tiers of pale stone houses, farm buildings below. On the slopes leading up to them, vineyards and olive groves; good cover, at least while the sun was low. Fran says he watched the village through field glasses before the light faded: crawling with Germans.

He watched Ash, too; his conversations with the major, the other platoon commanders. Taut expression on his too-young face, eyes anxious or angry, Fran couldn't decide. Made him nervous to look at him, and the assault seemed a long time in planning. Two platoons, including Fran's, were to take the farm on the eastern edge; three others were to approach the village from the west. Secure the lower tier, and they would have the backup in place to take the upper. These were the orders they got eventually, but meantime no word was given, nothing happened. It got dark, Fran slept. Quieter out there than in the hospital.

— In the morning, again no movement. Not for a whole day, as I remember.

Rifle cleaning, waiting. A seeming endless back-and-forth between Ash and the major, the commanders farther back in the field; only the signalmen kept busy. The sun set again.

— Dusk and dawn you were always edgy.

And when they passed there was no relief, he says, just the dull uncertainty of what was still to come. The shapelessness of it.

— I expected that, of course: not being told things.

They were often sent out not knowing much, but Fran insists this wasn't blind obedience, not for the most part. They were always guessing, interpreting, trying to slot their orders into a greater pattern. It was instinctive somehow, but unsettling, too, this incessant filling-in of the gaps. He didn't like rumors; couldn't help but listen to them. Heard someone asking Butler were they waiting for the tanks.

— As I remember it, Butler didn't answer.

Fran was always terrified by the fighting. Says he's not ashamed to admit it. But he shifts in his chair while he tells me, eyes on the trim horizon of hedge outside his window. So he was frightened, yes, but it was a relief when they finally got moving.

Two hours till dawn. Out of the woods onto the hillside, through the olives and into the vines. Keeping low, moving quickly, Fran remembers what the platoon looked like ahead of him, stooped figures filling the narrow avenues; the low noise they made together, breath and boot. The sky was blue-gray on the eastern horizon and they were making good ground; just beyond the farm buildings when he heard it.

— Shell.

Like a bird singing, or a whistle. Stuttering. High in the air but coming closer. Fran was flat on the ground when the explosions started. Heard gunfire, too, coming from somewhere. Fran lay shocked and still against the cool earth, until the sergeant screamed at him to start fucking shooting. And he did, but didn't know at what; green of the vines in front of him, knotted wood twisted along the wires.

Noise gets in everywhere, he explains. Blinds, somehow; confuses.

— So they had us with the shelling. Fierce. Seems obvious now, but we weren't expecting it.

His gun jammed, Thorn was next to him, the village above, and while Fran struggled to get his bearings he heard the order to move. The men ahead were running uphill, bent forward, low to the ground. Fran was following when he heard Thorn shout behind him. A shell landed: a tug in the earth as it erupted, raining soil, something harder. Fran missed his footing, remembers falling, not landing. Flung downhill. It was still dark, but he could see the shape of Thorn, struggling: down the slope where they were shooting. Terrible to be there, terrifying. Smoke and sharp torn leaf smell, tin and uniform between bullet and skin. He didn't want to, but Fran slid toward him. Thorn's arms were reaching forward, legs kicking at the earth, but he was held, mouth open, trapped in the wire.

— Push yourself up. Fucking push yourself up.

But Thorn didn't hear him.

— And the shelling goes on all this time.

Fran had hold of the wire, saw the buckle snagged, Thorn's weight dragging it down. Fran knew he had to lift him to pull the buckle clear, but Thorn kept moving, twisting away from him, slipping then sagging, snapping the wire taut against Fran's palms. Too quick to hurt, he says. He just remembers his grip sliding when the blood started, then the panic. He shouted, kicked Thorn onto his knees, and the buckle sprang free of the vines. Thorn was loose and he dropped, rolled away from Fran downhill under the dark leaves. The shelling went on and the other men had gone. Thorn was not moving now. Fran turned uphill and ran.

It was still dull blue in the tight spaces between the village buildings, sun not yet clear of the eastern ridges.

The shells were hitting roof and wall, too close, and he couldn't seem to move in the noise, it slowed everything down. Through a doorway out of the dawn, into a barn, dark and empty. Outside a shell struck. He still heard the high note of metal on stone before the bang, then nothing. The shock wave ran through him: silent air. Fran remembers standing in the sudden light and seeing beyond broken wall and gray-bright twisted shards: Before him was Ash, shouting, silent, and cellar steps. Fran stood, then obeyed; ran down them.

He doesn't know how long it took before he could hear again. Could feel the shells bursting before noise returned, the walls above them shifting. Sounds were shattered, painful cracks inside his head. He held his hands against his ears, and the blood from his palms dried on his cheeks. It was bright daylight outside; dusty shafts of it came through the gaps in the door at the head of the steps. The air was hot and close. There were four of them down there, including Ash and Butler. Over fifty came up. Fran remembers thinking they must be somewhere. Wondering who else was lying in the vines.

When the shelling let up awhile, Ash and Butler climbed into the room above, where there was a narrow window. Machine guns all along the top wall, Butler told him.

— Our mortar platoon had taken out a couple, but there were plenty more.

Ash was silent. No radio contact. He told Fran to see

to his hands, left the cellar with Butler behind him, and soon after that the shelling started up again.

— What will we do?

Fran knew the face next to him, but the name was gone. His palms ached, the ragged lines of sticky black where the wire cut in; he wrapped his field dressing around them. The man next to him was retching. Fran looked away, didn't want him to think he was watching. Remembers how his own stomach was sour and clenching.

It went on that way for hours. Endless noise, pain in his head and hands. He could hear them sometimes, in the few quiet minutes, the people still living there, the villagers. Three or four different voices, calling, crying. Couldn't understand what they were saying, heard English voices, too. Shouting for the stretcher bearers. He recognized the retching man, then. His stretcher propped up against the cellar wall and his legs laid out in front of him, twisted.

He doesn't remember how long they were down there, kept thinking someone might come for him, stripped his gun down, got the mechanism working, then his hands started bleeding again. The noise stopped toward evening and it wasn't until the light faded that he really thought it might be over. The stretcher bearer was unconscious so he climbed out alone.

Up in the village, there were bodies on the streets he recognized. The major was there already and Ash, Butler. Men that had taken the western approach and from the mortar platoons that had stayed below. No tanks.

The Germans retreated, they told him. Said it like they couldn't quite believe it themselves, but they were gone. Apart from three prisoners. Old men with gray hair and Iron Crosses. They sat quietly in a truck, waiting, nodding; talking in murmurs to the corporal guarding them.

Fran was sent to the dressing station. He waited outside the long building that he thinks must have been somebody's house. Inside were men with gunshot and shrapnel wounds, some dying, the stretcher bearer among them. It was almost dark. The old people in the village came out into the streets and put flowers on the corpses.

Tea and food and painkillers and sleep. Fran remembers telling the orderly about Thorn, who said that the padre would find him. His palms were cleaned and dressed. They hurt but he could hold his gun. The wounded were driven back to the coast. Fran was among those who moved farther north in the morning.

— It wasn't the worst I'd experienced. It wasn't that.

The mugs of tea Fran made have skinned over on the low table between us. He stirs his but doesn't drink. Tells me he'd seen dead before. Cleared away corpses, blackened in the sun. He'd killed and been shot.

— Like being hit by a hammer.

In a way he was lucky. The cuts on his hands weren't bad, his ears were recovering, the cellar had probably been the safest place in the village. Fran pauses, looks down at his tie, his trousers, shoes. When he doesn't speak, I count up the reasons he's given already. He was young, he'd been ill, morale was low. Thorn, the only man he knew in his platoon, had died in front of him, and the shelling had been horrific.

Fran shrugs after I've finished speaking. Says perhaps they do all have a part to play: Or perhaps that's just memory, arranging things in the mind again.

They were on a road, following the line of the ridgeway. Two trucks, canvas sides flapping. Dry earth track, dusty, the truck ahead throwing up clouds of dirt which they drove through. The ridgeway was not yet secured, so they were to join with other platoons, a day ahead. Together there might be enough of them to make up a full battalion.

They were sick, a lot of them. The runs, throwing up.

— We'd won a battle but it didn't feel like that.

Just degraded, somehow, humiliated. Leaning out over the sides of the truck, squatting in the undergrowth at the edge of the track.

It was normal to feel uneasy the day after. Most men would crawl into themselves awhile, if they had the chance to, if they didn't have to fight on. Fran said he could see it in the other men's faces, the strain, and he knew that feeling, but that day he felt different. Not calm exactly, no. He searches for a way to explain.

— Like being suddenly high up on a clear day, is how I would describe it.

Set apart from the other men, standing there, watching: unable to slot himself back in again. And the questions just kept coming.

— Why did the Germans retreat?

He found a seat in the truck beside Butler. He had been up in the village with Ash, might know something.

— You're asking me?

But he did know, or had heard another rumor. Something happened, somewhere else: another, more important place along the line. Germans got the order to pull back to where they were stronger.

— Nothing to do with us. We were fucked. Fucking lucky.

— No tanks came.

Fran remembers how Butler looked at him.

— You don't say.

The track was rough, narrow in places, and they made slow progress. Fran didn't like to look ahead any longer, eyes preferring the land they had left behind. Below the road, the slope fell away in terraces, olive groves, and at the bottom was a river, running along the valley floor. He remembers looking at it often that morning, and noticing how other men did the same. Checking, reassuring. Swift glances down the valley to the river.

— All of us.

Finding the line of retreat. Calculating how long it would take to get back. Watching the water flowing steadily south and west to the floodplain. Held by the British. Safe ground.

Midday and they stopped to eat. Fran kept close to Butler under the trees.

— Of course he knew. The major. There was no one coming for us.

— He knew they would shell us like that?

— Probably. We go and die, we're creating a little distraction. It worked, you might say. Retreated, didn't they?

Didn't talk much after that, Fran says. Smoked a lot, everybody did. Blue cloud under the branches, shady ground littered with stubs. Fran couldn't stop thinking about Ash and the major, couldn't take his eyes off the valley. Felt he was detaching inside, moving farther away all the time. Here the terraced olives led like giant steps down to a house with a walled garden, sitting alone in the country, where the valley leveled out before the river. And once he had noticed that house, all Fran could think about was how he could make it down there without being seen.

Terraces about shoulder height, he could stoop, maybe bend at the knees. He couldn't run very fast like that, but he wouldn't have to crawl. The trees were heavy with fruit, dense green-gray leaves. Trunks split and twisted, branches reaching low to the dry grass. Fran says he imagined the blue sky seen through twig and leaf. Could picture it all already: what he would see if he were hiding beneath them. He let himself plan it, didn't try to stop the thoughts, even when he saw Butler watching. His eyes sharp, face smeared, pale dirt gone dark with sweat.

The men climbed back into the trucks and Fran stayed back in the bushes. Pretended even to himself he was looking for a place to shit. Surprised at how easy it was, but not at all surprised to find Butler had stayed with him.

Clear of the road they stopped. Sat in the shadow of the first tier. Backs to the hill, they listening to the truck engines receding along the road above them. Fran checked over his shoulder. Couldn't see them, figured he couldn't be seen. When he turned back, Butler had already gone. He scrambled down the hill after him.

— Not that I want to say I followed him.

Or that he wouldn't have done it on his own: Never blame another man.

They slept in the dusty rooms with the broken windows. When they woke the sun was getting low and they ate carrots dug from the kitchen garden, bitter lettuces that had gone to seed, dry-sour apples picked too early from the trees. Butler found wine in the cellar, pushed the corks in with his thumbs.

— Ash is all right.

— But he sent us up there.

Fran heard the tears in his throat and hated them. Saw Butler's smile, mocking. His teeth wine-black: hated him.

— He didn't send us when he got the order. He delayed, remember? Maybe he got a lot of us killed, but then maybe

Ash is the one that saved us. You and me. Couple more hours, couple more of us left over.

It was all so obvious; it didn't seem worth crying about. Fran avoided Butler, lay in the cool shadow of the garden wall with the sun setting behind him, the sunburn flaking from his shoulders and arms.

— I was angry, I suppose you could say.

That someone had taken such a risk with his life. But then, he says there was little room for anger amidst all the platitudes. You were there to kill or be killed. Both, most likely. You saw death every day, and that it was random. No reason or pattern: Most died, some didn't. He couldn't even say for certain that they were lied to about the tanks. At most, they had been allowed to find comfort in the rumors.

— I just wanted no more part of it.

Fran sits up straight. He squints out of the window briefly and then says he had no sense of just cause, no idea at the time.

— What the Germans had been doing.

And then he shakes his head.

— Listen to me. Making excuses.

Even if he had known then, he doesn't think it would have stopped him.

— It was a cool calculation.

If they were going to send him up a hill to die, he would find a way round it.

It got dark. Neither of them could sleep properly. Fran

remembers seeing Butler standing on the terrace, looking up the line of the ridge, trying to guess where their battalion was. That they filled their water bottles together at the well, took more wine for the journey.

It was just after midday when they found the camp, and the men were eating. They hadn't talked about what they would say, if they would try to justify or lie. He remembers Butler smiling.

— Temporarily AWOL, sir. Back now.

The look of disbelief on Ash's face.

— Disgust, too. Like he hated us.

They were transferred, separately. North Africa, again, but not on leave this time: hard labor. Butler was court-martialed, Fran discharged, a few weeks after war's end. Dishonorable.

Deserter. Not shot like they were in the Great War. Fran remembers the other men's faces, when they turned up again. Is sure many of them thought they should have faced the firing squad.

— The road was mined, you see.

Five more men dead, and he and Butler had missed it by going cross-country.

Fran pauses there, blinking slowly. I think he might have finished, but I don't want to be the first to break the silence, so I wait. I can't see behind his glasses if he is crying. I wonder if I want him to be. And then why, exactly.

— Three from the first truck, two from the second. The one I was in.

Fran looks at me. Voice steady as he tells me he is sorry they died. That he has thought of them often: when he was in prison and in all the decades since. But stronger than the regret, even now, is the relief that he wasn't among them.

SECOND BEST

Ewa is early. Adela said she was to wait for them on the main road out of town and they would pick her up at ten o'clock, where the concrete was laid for the service station the summer before last. Ewa has six weeks' clothing zipped into a bag and twenty minutes to wait. Here the houses peter out into the surrounding country: heavy fields and a thin row of trees at the near horizon. The spring has been wet and the weeds grow thick, green-dark in the cracks of the unused forecourt. Few cars pass, a few people gather at the junction, watching for the morning coach that comes and then goes. The people say their good-byes and hellos, linger in small groups, disperse. Ewa stands alone, on the other side of the road, waiting.

East of the German border now, she will be south of Berlin soon, where the ground is more sand than soil. Asparagus land. Even in the city, Ewa knows, you can feel it under your feet: the grit that blows across the back courts and pavements, the city streets. She has not been

160

there, but she has heard tell, has been picturing it for weeks, ever since Adela suggested the job. Spring harvest: asparagus for the German capital. Six weeks of bending and cutting. Seven days, long hours, no matter. The more work, the more money, the better. And a two-month visa.

Adela is late, Ewa sits down on her bag. At the far end of the street she sees her sister coming, and that she has Jacek with her. Ewa groans as she sees the bicycle round the corner: Dorota pedaling, Jacek on the handlebars, sullen. Today nothing has gone according to plan.

— Adela called.

Dorota shouts as soon as she is in earshot.

— They have to change one of the wheels on the car. They'll get here as soon as they can.

Ewa stands as her sister pulls up in front of her. She tries to catch her son's eye, but he slips off the handlebars, keeps his face turned away. Ewa has said good-bye to him once already this morning, thinks Dorota has brought him deliberately, to make the whole thing harder.

— We wanted to keep you company.

Ewa nods and Jacek takes the bike and cycles a wide arc around his mother and aunt. Across the broken concrete of the forecourt, out into the road and back, circling. Legs too short for the saddle, he stands on the pedals, arms reaching forward and up to the handlebars. Ewa speaks to him as he turns.

— Just this month and next month, remember, then

the rent is paid and I'll come home. And you know, maybe we can even get a bicycle. A bicycle in time for summer, Jeżyku.

He pedals on and on. Ewa turns to her sister, and Dorota kisses her, but her grip on her arm is tight.

— I know what you are doing.

Ewa blinks. She kisses her sister back. No hiding anything from her.

— You went to see Piotr's mother.

Ewa wonders, briefly, if it is worth denying, worth lying, and then Jacek passes.

— You went to see the old sow.

— Don't talk about your grandmother like that, Jacek.

Ewa looks from her son to Dorota, who shrugs.

— I saw you there. This morning.

Ewa sighs.

— And so you told Jacek, of course.

— I'm not going to lie to him.

— Whose son is he?

— She'll be my mama while my mama is in Germany.

Jacek is still cycling. Dorota blushes. Ewa laughs.

— And you told him that, too, I suppose?

The two young women look at each other. They both have red hair, dyed red-brown and grown long around their pale faces.

— I want to go, Dorota. I want to earn some money for us, for me and Jacek. And I want to go to Berlin, too. See Piotr. See what he says.

The boy cycles up and down the empty forecourt behind them. Picking up speed, slamming on the brakes, trying to make the back wheel skid out on the concrete. Every so often he succeeds and then he shouts to his mother and she waves. The rest of the time she talks or stands in silence with her sister. They share a cigarette and when they speak, they mirror each other's movements. Shoulders shrugging in emphasis, thumbnail rubbing a lower lip.

— She wouldn't give me his address in Berlin, the old sow. She didn't even ask after Jacek. Just nothing, you know.

She takes an envelope out of her bag, shakes it so her sister can hear the coins inside, and then describes how her father-in-law threw it down to her as she was leaving. She was on the path up to the road when she heard him whistling, saw him lean out the toilet window in his vest.

— I didn't even know the old man was at home. Must have been in the bathroom the whole time. The only room in that flat with a lock, you know. And now it's just him and the old girl, I think he shuts himself away in there.

Jacek shouts, Dorota waves, Ewa smiles, opens the envelope, shows her sister: thirty-three deutschmarks and Piotr's address.

— I don't think it's a good idea, Ewa.

— I know you don't.

Adela arrives, an hour later than planned. Small car loaded with suitcases and boxes, other asparagus cutters: Adela's brother Marek and two cousins. They make room for Ewa on the backseat while she pushes her bag into the boot.

Her son stops cycling and watches her.

— I'm going now, Jeżyku. Time to say good-bye again.

He stands astride Dorota's bicycle on the other side of the forecourt, at the far edge where concrete gives way to mud, then field. Ewa waves to him but he doesn't come over. Stock still, blue T-shirt and long pale hair. He stares and Ewa calls, laughing at first, but then saying come on, and please.

— Jacek. Please?

There is a short silence in which they both stand and blink, mother and son. And then Jacek turns: drops the bicycle and runs. Fast, without looking back, disappearing as the road curves south into the town. Leaving Ewa with the abandoned bicycle, and the clicking, spinning motion of its upturned wheel.

In the car, the others are kind. Pressed together, they pretend not to notice that Ewa is crying. She stares out at the fields passing, Poland going, Germany coming, feels the tears dry on her cheeks, tight and itchy. Only another hour or two, and they will be on the farm already, and tomorrow they will start working. She will earn some money and then she'll go looking. In her pocket, Ewa has a Berlin address. No phone number. And it's good that way. She doesn't want to call him. No warning.

Dorota is tempted, but she doesn't tell Jacek what his mother will do when she gets her wages. Over there, on the other side of the border. Even though it takes her two hours to find him after Ewa has gone and he shows no sign of being sorry. Even though she has to keep the salon closed all morning because of him and the customers are angry. Even when he kicks the table legs and refuses his dinner, and the already small kitchen becomes much smaller, and her husband, Tadeusz, picks up his plate and goes to eat standing outside in the stairwell. Even then Dorota respects her sister's wishes and bites her tongue.

When Piotr left, he never told her, never said that he wanted to go. Dorota has never known whether to believe this entirely, but it's what Ewa always insisted. She turned up at their place with Jacek and two bags one morning, told them Piotr had been gone for three days already.

Ewa didn't cry, though Jacek did all the time. For weeks it was just about impossible to get a word out of her. All she said was that he'd written a letter: The postmark was still Poland, but one of the towns at the border.

Inside he told them he was gone, but not where to or how long he would stay there.

— He never said why? He never gave you the least indication?

Ewa put her hands over her face when Dorota started shouting, spoke from beneath her palms in a quiet monotone. She checked through his things, she said, while she was packing. In the wardrobe, the drawers, the laundry basket, under the mattress. She couldn't find anything, and only one change of clothes was missing.

He'd lost his job, of course, the winter before, but then so had well over a hundred others in the town when the bottling plant closed. They hadn't gone, at least not so soon, and at least when they did, they sent money to their families, promised to come home. It was not an easy time, not for anyone, but they'd seen worse, surely. The elections had been, they had a new government, a whole new system, and it was bound to be painful for a while, but it made no sense to her to leave: not now that everything was changing.

Dorota tried to understand them. Not only Piotr, but also her sister: why she was so quiet, why she never asked any questions. Tadeusz found Ewa the first of a series of jobs: evenings with his brother at the bakery. And then a couple of rooms in a building nearby that weren't too expensive. In that first time, money was often short, and they would do their best to help her. Dorota sat for Jacek a couple of times a week, and would try to talk to her sister when she came home from work. But Ewa just used to say:

— Another time, yes? I'm tired, okay?

And then she would climb into the bed beside her boy, ask Dorota to turn the light off when she was ready to go.

It was spring then, and cool and wet, just like now. Jacek was two, they had been married nearly three years, and Ewa was barely twenty.

Dorota thinks Ewa wants to know now. And she doesn't blame her.

It rains the first week on the farm, almost without stopping. But it is warm and the asparagus tips push their way up through the fine soil, pale combs sprouting along the dark tops of the trenches.

It is hot work, Ewa bending, crouching, digging with her left hand, forcing the knife down into the earth with her right. Twenty of them, making their way along the rows, the farmer teaching those who are new, then working alongside them. He speaks only a few words of Polish, the necessary ones, explains methodically, by demonstration, drawing the fat yellow-white asparagus spears up out of the sandy soil. Ewa gets faster, the stems she pulls longer: She learns to anticipate the snap and release as she works the blade through. Sweat gathers in drops on her back, underneath her breasts, mixes with the cooler rain which runs from her cheeks, down her throat, off the nape of her neck. Water inside and out. By the end of the first hour each day, her coat is wet, her jumper dry, the T-shirt beneath soaked through.

While she works, she thinks about her sister. That Dorota has probably been waiting for her to do this for months now. Ever since the divorce papers arrived from Berlin. But then winter came, Christmas, and another year, and Ewa said nothing, did nothing; life went on as normal. She could see Dorota was suspicious, of course, when Adela's idea came up and Ewa said she would go to Germany with her. But when Dorota challenged her about it, Ewa was always careful not to give a straight answer. Sometimes she'd claim she had signed the papers, sent them back to the lawyers.

— Weeks ago already.

Other times she'd say she had lost them, torn them up, made them into papier-mâché for a school project with Jacek. And when Dorota complained about being lied to, Ewa would just shrug.

— Don't ask, then.

She thinks how Dorota can be hard work: never seems to know when to stop, always wants her answers immediately, doesn't understand the need for time to think things over. But Ewa has to smile when she thinks of her, and she does wonder if it's fair to treat her sister the way she does, after the way Dorota has helped her. Ewa's palms itch in the hot gloves so she takes them off, stuffs them in her pockets. The wet sand and soil work their way under her nails, leave her fingertips raw, stinging in the morning when she wakes up in the dormitory.

Dorota walks Jacek to school early, mostly in silence. Her head full of questions she is not sure about asking, Jacek's mouth set, his eyes averted, so she can't tell what he might be thinking about, if he's thinking about anything.

Jacek never talks about him, so Dorota doesn't know if he thinks about his father, what he remembers of him. She calculates: seven now, born in the spring before the elections, so about five years now since he's seen him. Dorota can't be sure what Ewa has told her son, what she hasn't. Why Piotr left, never came back, why they didn't go with him.

Jacek says a hurried good-bye at the corner and then runs ahead so she can't take him right to the gate. Dorota stops. She waits until he has crossed the strip of playground and she can see he has gone inside, and then she walks on. Past the school building on her way to the salon.

All day as she cuts, dries, and washes, Dorota tries to assess what would be appropriate to tell a seven-year-old about his parents, to anticipate his questions. In the absence of answers, she confuses them with her own:

whether Ewa still loves his father, whether she wants them back together, back in Poland, or all three living, illegally, in the German capital.

She has no idea.

Dorota also doesn't know if she could simply tell Jacek facts: not without her voice slanting them this way or that. She tries it out a few times, lying in bed at night, and her husband tells her no, no.

— You still sound like you disapprove.

Tadeusz sighs and reaches out and rubs her belly before he goes to sleep. And Dorota lies awake a long time, still trying to work things out.

Ewa's days pass quickly. The work is monotonous, but the place more interesting than she thought, and the people. The farm is small, and when they arrived, the farmer made a point of telling them that his place was family run: different from the larger farms that own the land all around. He pointed as he spoke, made a wide arc with his arm. He has three children. He and his wife and the eldest, a daughter, often work with them.

Lunchtime, and they eat all together, hired hands and the family, the farmer's daughter serving thick soup, long sausages, and small white rolls. The girl is sixteen, maybe seventeen, with fair hair and spots. Looks like her mother, moves with the same even gestures as her father. Ewa takes the bowl she offers, finds a place to sit between Adela and her brother. This is Marek's fifth asparagus year, his third here. Adela said he was friendly with the farmer, and Ewa is curious.

— Was this part of a collective before, when she was born?

Ewa points to the daughter with her spoon. Marek nods, chewing. Adela answers for him.

— Her grandfather stayed out as long as he could, but they forced him in the end.

Marek swallows, joins in.

— He couldn't get loans, machines, fertilizer. They called him an enemy of the people, the party functionaries. It divided the village. Still does, her father says.

Farmer and daughter are carrying the soup pots to the deep sink, collecting empty bowls from their workers. Marek takes a last bite of his bread, speaks with his mouth full.

— He took the land back again, after the wall fell, soon as he could. Wants it to go to her later, keep it in the family, out of the privatized collectives. He says the spirit of eighty-nine is still alive here. Fighting for the subsidies from Brussels.

Marek winks at her. Outside it is drizzling and they pull their hoods up and boots on again. Ewa's are a size too large and her heels slide up into the legs as she walks across the yard. The daughter comes out to the fields with them in the afternoon, and Ewa watches her cutting: more and faster than any of them, her father included. Eyes elsewhere, soft face closed.

It rains on the other side of the border too, and Jacek runs home after school. His legs carry him without thinking past the church and fire station to the two rooms he has shared with Ewa as long as he can remember, and it is only when he gets to the kiosk at the corner that he realizes what he's done. He doesn't turn immediately but stands a moment at the edge of the pavement, where the telephone wires cross overhead. His hood is pulled tight around his face and he can hear his own breath. Dorota's salon is ten minutes in the other direction.

She watches for him at the window. Two clients have canceled because of the weather and now Jacek is late coming from school. When she finally sees him, he is walking slow, stiff-legged in rain-soaked trousers. Dorota goes to the small back room for towels, spreads a slice of bread and jam, which he takes from her wordlessly when he comes in. He sits down without taking his coat off and eats, swiveling the salon chair to the window so he can watch the few cars and people passing, the water running down the wide pane.

———

They are six in the dormitory: Ewa, Adela, and four other women. Two German and two from just outside Warsaw whom Adela knows already from last year. In the evenings they cook and eat together in the communal kitchen, Adela translating. Paula, one of the German women, has children and shows Ewa photos. Ewa has no picture of Jacek so she describes him.

— He's not the easiest. Such a boy, you know? But I love him.

They work late, are usually tired, sometimes play cards. Often they are in bed by ten. Lights out, the glow of Adela's cigarette in the dark, Ewa whispers with her in sleepy tones. She keeps the envelope in her bedside locker. Has told Adela the story about her father-in-law, leaning out of the fourth-floor bathroom window.

— What will you say when you see Piotr?

— I don't know.

— Do you want to be with him again?

— I don't know.

The women in the other beds listen, tease her.

— She's come to Germany to find a Polish man.

— Did no one tell her there are plenty in Poland already?

— Oh piss off, you two. Go to sleep.

Adela stabs out her cigarette in mock annoyance, Ewa lies in the dark and smiles.

She used to make love with her husband in the bathroom, when they lived at her in-laws' place. So she knows those four private walls, the lace curtains, and what you could see through them. Piotr would sit her up on the windowsill, when Jacek was asleep, his parents out working. Afterward she would keep her arms around him, and they would press their faces to the curtain and glass, watch the wind in the trees outside through the gaps in the net pattern. Piotr would sleep like that sometimes. Standing and leaning into her and the window. And she would watch his breath mist the pane, know the net was leaving its flowery imprint on his cheek and on her shoulder.

Jacek didn't want to speak to Ewa when she called last night and so Dorota listened to her sister crying on the phone until her money ran out. She is still angry with Jacek when he comes to the salon after school. Lets him spread his own bread with jam, leaves him to get on with his homework in the small back room. Later, after she locks up, she presents Jacek with a clean rag and a bottle of vinegar to polish the mirrors. Dorota sweeps the day's hair up, and because he is quiet, she talks to him.

— Our parents were old, so they died when we were young, you see.

— Mmm.

— I was married, but your mama was just fifteen. She knew your father then already.

Jacek sprays the mirror and Dorota doesn't know if he is listening. She sweeps on in silence awhile, not sure what she wants to say, what it is exactly she wants her nephew to understand. That Ewa was too young to know better, still is? She hears the tones of judgment in her own thoughts and flushes, jabbing at the soft gray-brown pile she has gathered with her broom. Her sister is twenty-five now, was an eighteen-year-old bride, and the idea still shocks her. But Tadeusz, Father Gregory, Aunt Jasia: Everyone told her Ewa should marry. As quickly as possible. Piotr had just done his national service, Ewa was still at school, but even her teachers and Piotr's parents would call on Dorota about it. They didn't say it, of course, but the urgency was there in their voices: before she gets pregnant. And then, when Jacek was born a little over eight months later, the same people nodded, how fortunate it was that they hadn't waited. Dorota watches Jacek rub the vinegar smears dry on the glass and remembers crying the morning of Ewa's wedding: relief and regret. And afterward, that she went with her sister to the housing office to put her married name on the waiting list, for the flat they never got. Even after Jacek came along and the new government and they thought everything would get better. Ewa moved to her in-laws' in the meantime, and then out again nearly three years later. Not long after Piotr.

— I know my father is in Berlin.

Dorota looks up.

— Do you remember him?

Jacek blinks.

— Will you cook soon, or do we have to wait for Tadeusz to come home?

The weather turns cold, and the wind blows in hard from home, driving the rain east to west in sheets across the fields. The asparagus stops growing.

There is other work to do, washing, sorting, bunching, packing, but the farmer's wife says there isn't room in the barn for all of them, so they are to work in two shifts. One in the morning, the other in the afternoon: They can divide the work amongst themselves and the first group will start in two hours. Ewa dresses while the others make themselves coffee and comfortable, get back into bed for a while. She offers Paula, the German mother, her shift, says she needs a day off, and Paula giggles, puzzled, until she understands Ewa's sign language, then she nods gladly. Adela is in the shower and Ewa pulls on her coat as she opens the door: leaving before Adela can stop her. She walks the path between the fields to the road, back to the wind, landscape ahead of her blurred. The long, parallel lines of the asparagus trenches lead her eye to gray nothingness, no horizon visible, just rain.

The farmer sits in his van, eating his breakfast roll, watching her standing where the track joins the road north, under the sign to the city, occasionally holding out her thumb. The few cars which pass ignore her, and the farmer judges from the way the trees are bending, and how she draws her hood close around her cheeks, that the rain and spray must be blowing full in her face.

Ewa stays there almost half an hour before she starts walking. And the farmer stays there, too, radio on, windscreen misting. And when Ewa is out of sight, he looks out across the asparagus fields, the long, pale strips of polythene covering the sandy rows. Knows the stubborn white crowns are nestled somewhere beneath the surface. Unwilling to grow into the wind which has him gripping the steering wheel when it catches the high sides of the van.

Ewa waited half an hour, walked for two. One hour north and another hour back south again. Back to the women in the dormitory, who don't say anything when she appears, blue-lipped and dripping, but wake her up later with coffee and biscuits, and make her cups of sweet black tea in the morning when her head hurts and her bones ache and her eyes are gummed together.

When the farmer comes to say they will do the same half-day shift pattern, Adela clears it with him in her good German and low voice that Ewa should stay in bed. He says he will get his daughter to bring some aspirin.

In the afternoon, the rain slows and the wind drops. Ewa gets up and walks across to the barn where the others are sorting. She works on into the evening, after the others have gone inside to wash and cook. Only Marek stays with her, sifting the stringy root and stalk into crates ready for planting.

Ewa has known Adela since school, her family too. Started sitting next to her in class the same year martial law was declared, when they were ten, eleven. Adela was the youngest in her family, Marek her oldest brother. She came to school on a winter morning and whispered to Ewa that he had gone, but Ewa was to say nothing. She remembers thinking how sad it was, that he had to leave then, because it was just before Christmas. Marek was married, to loud Feliksa with the gray eyes, and they already had two children. Adela's mother would send her to help Feliksa after school and sometimes Adela invited Ewa to go with her. They would cook or play with the babies, or go out and queue if Feliksa had had no luck at the shops in the morning. It didn't seem sad that Marek was gone then, more exciting: a husband in the underground and later in prison. Ewa hoped, expected, that one day she'd have one of her own. Marek was a photo beside Feliksa's pillow, a rumor that turned up in the night and was gone again: for years at a time. Ewa remembers when they heard about him being arrested that, despite everything, it was somehow thrilling. And then later, how she'd boasted, to impress Piotr, that she knew him.

Marek was released after the amnesty. He came to

their wedding, a year or two later, and people said he was ill, that he had changed: unrecognizable. Adela got angry when Ewa told her, said he'd done enough, just wanted be left alone now, with his family. The democracy he had gone to prison for arrived in hard-fought stages, but he said he'd rather leave the strikes and rallies to the younger men; had three more children with Feliksa in the years after he came home. Now Konrad, the middle one, goes to school with Jacek, and Marek comes to work in Germany with his little sister and her friend from school. He stacks his completed crates on the floor, smiling at Ewa as he starts on another set.

— Deutschmarks for our boys.

The fluorescent tubes hum over the long tables, the rain falls steadily, soft against the dark skylight. Ewa watches Marek, hands working, a constant motion in front of his soft belly. The skin under his eyes is loose, hairline receding. When she and Adela got a bit older, fourteen, fifteen, Feliksa had told them about him, sitting around the kitchen table on their after-school afternoons. A shared cigarette, a half glass each of something strong, and tales of what it was like to sleep with Marek, what she missed now he was gone, and what she didn't. That he had cried in front of her, the night the phones went dead and the message came that the other union men were being arrested. Now, as she works and watches him, Ewa thinks how frightened he must have been: How perverse it was, that she had thought it romantic. But they had been her ideal: Lonely Feliksa, Absent Marek: the sacrifices they made in the hope of a better life for all of them.

Feliksa works now, taught herself bookkeeping, took a correspondence course in computing, and Marek seems to like being at home to take care of their young ones. Ewa collects Jacek from them sometimes, if he goes home with Konrad after school, and she enjoys being in the familiar flat again, likes the way Marek cooks dumplings, much better than the ones she and Adela made for Feliksa in the same kitchen, all those years ago. Back then, she often tried to imagine what the better life would look like, after the sacrifices were over. And she smiles now, because she knows this picture would never have occurred to her: she and Marek sitting in a German barn together, sorting asparagus into bundles.

Ewa doesn't see the farmer come in, only notices him when he stops at the trestle opposite. Marek stands, and they shake hands and talk to each other, partly in German, partly in Russian. Ewa listens to them: grown men speaking a language they learned at school, both Eastern bloc children once, both about the same age perhaps. She watches the two men talking, smiling, and remembers something Adela told her: that the farmer always asks for Marek personally now, when he applies for seasonal workers at the employment service.

— It is late.

The farmer is looking at Ewa; he says it in Russian

and it takes Ewa a couple of seconds to understand, to hear the words through his German accent. She smiles, nods, has not spoken Russian since her final exams: tries.

— This morning in bed. So I work now.

— You want to go to Berlin?

Ewa blinks. Wonders who told him, if he saw her go, perhaps. His tone is neutral, he doesn't seem angry about the missed day's work, but Ewa thinks it best to make sure he understands.

— I left my paper blank yesterday. No pay.

— Yes, yes, I know.

He waves a dismissive palm.

— From tomorrow the weather will be good again, so we will cut lots this week, I think.

— Yes.

— So then we can all have a day off perhaps. At the weekend. Marek can drive you to the station. You should get a train to Berlin from there, it is better than hitching.

The farmer is right. The days are warm and clear, they work long hours, the sun shines on into the evenings, and Ewa gets freckles across her nose and on her forearms. Piotr always liked them, and she hopes the hot weather holds, so they are still there when she finds him.

Getting used to the cutting routine, bodies adjusting, they are less tired, stay up later after they have eaten. Ewa plays chess sometimes, with Adela's cousins, and with

Artur, another cutter from Silesia, ex-miner, old colleague of Marek's, from his union days. They set up the boards on a rickety table out in the yard, and the late spring evenings are warm, moths battering themselves against the electric light on the side of the barn. Marek's friend is a good chess player, but she doesn't like the conversations they have afterward. He tells her he worked on a bigger farm last year where the pay was better.

— Should have gone back there, shouldn't have listened to Marek.

— Marek says it's much nicer here.

— Nice is cheaper. They cook us some lunch, we get to know their kids, they make a show of working with us, and then complaining about the wages starts to seem rude, doesn't it?

— They work just as hard, Artur, it's not a show.

— Yeah, yeah. And the farmer tells Marek how much he likes us Poles, the way we stick together, haven't sold our souls for freedom. Patronizing bullshit, and Marek falls for it.

— I think he's all right, the farmer. It's all right here.

— We're cheap labor, Ewa, from across the border, because their own people get more on the dole.

— You're not telling me anything I don't know.

Ewa tries to deflect Artur's cynicism with some of her own, but it gets to her all the same, makes the early mornings even more difficult, the long hours harder to take. Ewa does without the chess games, spares herself the aggravation, stays in the dormitory after the evening meal, talking: most often with Adela and Paula.

— She says she grew up near here, and they used to get days off school to help with the harvest. Potato fights in the fields in the autumn.

Adela lies on her back on the bed, translating what Paula tells them, smoking, eyes closed. Paula sits straight-backed on a chair by the open window, Ewa standing behind her, winding Paula's hair around her fingers, the heated tongs, as she has watched her sister do to so many women over the years.

— She moved to the West with her husband after re-unification, but they are divorced now.

Ewa smells the hair heating up, the oil and perfume in the mousse rising into the air. She can't do it as well as Dorota, but she tries, and she feels Paula relaxing, the hum of her voice, the stop-start rhythm of Adela's trans-lation. Life stories told in the last hours before sleeping.

— She thought she might look for permanent work, try to come back to live here with her children, but says she won't. The other farms here stayed in the collective, privatized now, with the same people running them, only half the workers. All her friends have gone, the place feels empty. And there are no jobs here anyway.

The evenings are over too quickly and no matter how she spends them, Ewa always ends them thinking about Piotr. Legs stretched long against each other under the blanket, skin to skin. Three years together in a single bed, no moving apart, even when she was pregnant. Piotr's sleeping breath on her shoulder, Jacek stirring and turning, getting comfortable under her skin.

Ewa knows she is being sentimental. Forces herself awake in her dormitory bed, correcting her own picture with memories of food prices out of control, and unpaid wages, the far too small flat shared with his parents. This was after Jacek was born, after the changes, and she remembers Piotr sitting on the edge of the bed, telling her things would get much, much worse before they had a hope of getting better.

— We have no privacy, nothing to look forward to.

He said this to her so often back then, she had been stupid not to see it coming.

Sunday and they are all sleepy. The day is bright-hot and blue and most of the cutters bring their breakfasts out into the yard, standing with eyes closed, chewing, faces tilted to the sky. Ewa washed her jeans last night, has the envelope from her father-in-law stuffed into the still-damp back pocket. Some of the others plan a trip to the lake to swim; Marek says he will drive Ewa to the station.

— Just one more coffee.

The car rattles over the cobblestones in the town and Ewa holds her door closed to keep the noise down a little. The Sunday streets are empty, all strong light on pale stone. Marek squints and yawns as he drives, eyes still puffy, he doesn't say much. She has been told such a lot about his marriage over the years, doesn't know what he knows about her own. That Piotr is in Berlin is common knowledge: When she found out, Ewa had the feeling that most people knew it already. And she thinks the reason for this little trip must be obvious to Marek, but if he is curious, he doesn't show it, and Ewa is grateful.

He comes into the station with her, helps her find the next direct service on the yellow timetable on the wall, a couple of potential times to come back on the white, and then he buys her a ticket.

— I'll pay you back.

— You don't have to. But I want you to use the return half, okay?

Jacek goes to church with Dorota and Tadeusz, a reassuring part of his normal routine. Even when his mother is at home, she doesn't go, but because all his school friends do, his aunt ended the arguments between him and Ewa by picking him up on Sunday mornings after breakfast, walking him there sometimes alone, sometimes with his uncle. Jacek enjoys the hushed echoes under the high roof; muffled coughs under the intonation of the sermon; shuffling coats in the line before communion; anticipating the swift, light touch of the priest's fingers.

Ewa used to take him to the church when he was younger: never to the service, but on weekday afternoons when it was quiet and empty. This was before he started school, and he was still quite small then, remembers how she used to sit him on one of the dark cushions in the pews along the side aisle, by the confessional. He could hear the low exchange after she went inside, but not the words spoken: soft pattern of murmur and silence making him sleepy.

Often, when he opened his eyes again, he would be in his mother's arms, and she would be walking. Out on the street, in the daylight, on the way somewhere else, and it would be good to be out of the dark and dust of the empty church, but still he remembers the shock of waking. She had come and lifted him away while he was dreaming, and then it always took a while to adjust, to get comfortable with his changed surroundings.

Sitting between aunt and uncle now, he remembers waking on one such afternoon. Not walking this time, but sitting on his mother's lap in the pews. She held him still when he wanted to move, one finger raised to touch her lips to warn him from talking. In front of them was a crying man, kneeling before the statue of Saint Jude. He was close, but didn't seem to have noticed them. He mouthed the words of his prayer on and on, eyes closed, tears falling, dropping from his chin, and Jacek sat leaning into his mother's chest with her arms close around him.

— Don't move, sweetheart, no noise. We don't want to disturb him.

Her own eyes swollen, the skin a light red tone around them.

The train comes into Berlin through the eastern suburbs. Past high-rise blocks painted mint green, egg yellow, along the wide expanses of track, past rusty sidings, weeds flowering white and lilac, growing tall between the sleepers. Ewa gets out at the first main-line station, as Paula told her to: She had recognized the postal code in Piotr's address, said it was in former East Berlin. But the Hauptbahnhof is not at all as she had described it: The surfaces in the wide concourse are all new, clean plastic and metal. Paula said they rebuilt it just before the wall came down: pride of the East German railway. Probably didn't know it was being rebuilt again, with a new entrance hall and a two-storey shopping center added. Most of the new shop fronts still stand empty, and Ewa wanders past them to the far end, where the renovations continue. Temporary signs and arrows direct the passengers through the dust and noise to alternative exit points. Ewa doesn't know where she should go, follows the largest stream of people to the main exit and out onto the street.

A wide road crosses here, and at the corner, she finds a newspaper kiosk selling maps. Standing, flicking through the booklet to the index, Ewa looks up for a street sign, to orient herself. She is on Mühlen Strasse, broad and roaring with traffic, and a long, high wall runs the full length of the pavement opposite. Covered in graffiti. Painted scenes, colors once bright, now peeling. Slogans, exclamation marks, symbols of peace and politics, flags and doves, reaching hands. Ewa stares at the flaking concrete, can't quite believe what she is seeing.

Turning the folds of the map, she finds a dotted red line which zigzags its way along and across the streets, cutting a path from north to east, then encircling the south and west of the folded paper city. Ewa recognizes enough of the words in the English legend at the front of the booklet: run of the former Berlin Wall. The dotted line cuts along the wide boulevard she is on, too, between the road and the wide river behind, so she thinks this must be it. A remainder, maybe two hundred meters of it. There are hardly any pedestrians here and the cars drive fast past the painted concrete façade, no stopping or looking. Farther down the street, though, Ewa can see a large coach, heavy, of the air-conditioned variety, and a couple of people standing awkwardly, laughing: one pretending to give the other a leg up over the wall, while a third takes a photo.

Ewa can't watch. She looks instead in the index, finds the grid code, and then Piotr's street on the map. It is over the next fold, and she follows the train lines with her fingers. Sees she will have to change once, twice: She goes back into the station.

———————

A quiet street of scraggy trees and five-storey tenements, crumbling and blackened façades, familiar from home, her visits to Adela when she was working in Krakow. Ewa crosses the road to number fourteen. The entry system is broken, wires hang from the wall, but Ewa tries the handle and the front door is open. She climbs the stairs, looking at the names on the buzzers: doesn't have a flat number on the note from her father-in-law. There is scrawl on the walls, but the floors are clean, still damp, and the stairwell smells of bleach and warm water, Sunday cooking.

Jerzy, the name Ewa tries is Polish, and the woman who answers the door is too. She listens while Ewa explains why she is there, holding the door half closed across her body.

— There is no one called Piotr living here.

— I got this address from his father.

The woman shrugs, looks briefly past Ewa down the stairwell, then back at her face.

— I'm not from the police or anything. I'm his wife.

The woman's eyes flicker a moment.

— Piotr never said he had a wife.

— Yes, well, he has a son, too.

Ewa can't keep the edge out of her voice.

— He doesn't live here now. He moved away about a year ago.

— In Berlin? Still in Berlin?

— I don't know.

— You don't?

Ewa looks at her, the woman relents.

— Yes. In Berlin.

And then:

— How old is your boy?

— Seven. Just turned seven. How can I find him? Piotr?

— I don't know. We're not in touch. He only lived here a couple of months.

— Do you know any of his friends?

— No.

— Nothing?

— Nothing.

Ewa sighs. She thinks she might cry. Instead she fumbles in her bag, tears a corner from the map she bought, writes down the number of the dormitory pay phone.

— I'd be very grateful. If you think of anything.

The woman takes the scrap of paper and Ewa thinks she watches her walking down the stairs, because she doesn't hear the door close behind her.

She takes a wrong turning at some point after she leaves the building, expects to come to the underground station, but finds herself instead on a small square with a large black church. Evangelical, not Catholic. She hesitates. The evening service will not begin for another hour at least, the doors are open.

It is plain inside, with long pale wood pews, a table for an altar, and the cross above it is empty. Large flower arrangements stand on either side of the aisle and the heavy smell of the lilies carries across to Ewa in the doorway.

No Saint Jude to pray to here, and Ewa smiles, thinks how Dorota hates it when she calls him her favorite and protector, patron saint of lost causes.

It is a long time since she has been in a church, of any kind. Couldn't bear the thought of people looking and knowing, in the services after Piotr left, so she stopped going. For six months perhaps, and then, when she tried again, she found that she just couldn't stand it. The suffering and piety, the demand that she put her faith in the Almighty. She did still go and see Father Gregory, though. Occasionally at first, then more regularly. Weekday afternoons for over a year, nearer two maybe. He was the one that had married them, and she would go and talk to him in the confessional. About Piotr, not about any sins she had committed: She didn't want to believe in those any longer, and told him so, which didn't stop him blessing her. Jacek would sleep in the pews outside and Father Gregory said she should be patient, that there would be more work again soon and then Piotr would come home, all of the others. Always the same answer and so Ewa stopped going: figured that if he believed in God, then to him probably anything was conceivable.

The last time she was in a church was for Father Gregory's funeral. She went only because Dorota cried when she said she wouldn't. It seems cruel to her now, hardhearted: He had listened while she spoke, and was kind when she cried, and he had been one of the few who stood up, said his piece for them, and that must have taken courage. Ewa remembers a service he gave, after the news came that Marek and some of the others had been arrested. No Piotr yet, so she must have been fourteen, not much older. The father spoke out in support of the men, their families, and of the union. His words were quiet, but they passed like a charge through the congregation. And afterward, people didn't go home as usual, but stayed in the church or the street outside; no one seemed to think about leaving.

Dorota was newly married then, and Ewa remembers finding her standing out on the steps with Tadeusz in the sun. His cheeks were flushed, eyes dark and glittering. One of the few times she had known her brother-in-law to be happy.

Outside the church a tram passes and Ewa is back in Berlin. She has no watch on, does not know what time it is: knows she should find where she is on the map, walk to the underground, get a train to the main-line station. But she doesn't want to move just yet, so she stays a few minutes longer. Sits alone in the pews and misses her family.

———

Late afternoon and Jacek is hauled back to the flat by a neighbor. She holds him at the door by a fistful of collar, tells Dorota she found him out behind the old bottling plant, smashing windows.

Dorota says she will have to tell Ewa, tonight when she phones, and that his mother will be unhappy: He will have made her unhappy, because she wanted him to be good while he stayed with her and his uncle. They are in the kitchen, and Dorota talks while she is cooking. Tadeusz reads the newspaper, and Jacek stands in the doorway, listening, sulking.

— She doesn't care.

— Yes she does. She will be very angry.

— She won't come back.

Dorota laughs, but it doesn't sound right: not light as she thought it would.

— Yes, she will. And then you'll be for it.

— She will go and see him and then they will both stay away.

— No.

— Tell her to come home.

— I can't do that, Jacek, she is working now. She needs to earn some money, you know that.

— No!

Jacek kicks the door, punches the door frame. Tadeusz frowns.

— Stop it.

And Jacek does stop, but only to turn to Dorota, mouth stretched wide and shouting.

— I hate you!

She stops chopping and looks at him. His eyes are wet, hands in fists, held clenched: white at the knuckles and raised level with his hips.

— Listen, Jacek. That's really not fair. I am just trying to do what's best for all of us.

— You make her come back, then!

His small face is red and torn with fury. Tadeusz looks up.

— It is hard, boy. Isn't it?

He doesn't stand up or go to Jacek to comfort him. Tadeusz stays in his chair at the kitchen table, still holding the two-day-old newspaper, still looking at the open pages as if he were reading them.

— But you can't bend the world to fit your plan, I'm afraid. None of us can.

Tadeusz nods at his nephew and goes back to his paper, and Jacek watches him a moment before he starts crying. Still standing in the kitchen doorway, he wraps his arms across his face. And then his shoulders, belly, knees jerk with the sobs that come and that he has no control over. He doesn't run away. And when Dorota goes to him and crouches, puts her arms around his waist, he stands rigid, unbending at first, but after a few minutes she feels him lean into her.

It is so good to hold the boy like this that Dorota wants to cry too, but she doesn't. She checks her breath and watches her husband, his eyes fixed on the newspaper, but not moving. And though she knows he has little time for Jacek and even less for Ewa, he will accept these weeks with their silences and shouting, and dinners eaten in the hallway. And then Dorota is glad of what she has, and thinks it is not so hard, really. She loves her sister, her nephew, her Tadeusz. She can sit out the spring.

Wait and see what happens.

When she gets off the train, Ewa calls the farm from the pay phone in the station building and then stands at the window opposite, waiting for Marek.

Evening, and on the small town square a group of teenagers sit on the benches, smoking. Wide trousers, loose sweatshirts, and acne, one or two with cans of beer, others drinking Pepsi. The girls smoke, long hair drawn back into tight ponytails; the boys wear theirs short, brushed forward, stiff and slick with gel.

Ewa wonders if they were all born here, if their families are farmers like the one she works for, or if their grandparents were the party functionaries who coerced and insulted. The village was divided, Marek had said, but he didn't say whether the families still fall into us and them, or if the lines have become blurred already in this youngest generation. Ewa knows one of her neighbors worked for the security service, has seen Jacek running with her children on the school playground occasionally, has never thought to stop him. She recognizes the farmer's daughter and waves. The girl's nod is barely perceptible, and she doesn't look at Ewa, fixing her gaze into the middle distance. Ewa moves away from the window, embarrassed. Sits on the bench beside the ticket office and tries not to think it is because she is Polish, tells herself it is unfair of the girl to jump to such conclusions. Jacek doesn't like to be walked to school now, will pretend not to see her if she passes one of his football games on the square behind the fire station.

She can still see the group through the window from where she is sitting. The skinny boys make her think of her son. *Six, seven years from now.* Provincial town kids in western Poland, in eastern Germany: There doesn't seem much to choose between them.

When Marek comes, the farmer's daughter ignores his wave too, but Marek just laughs.

— She'll grow out of it.

The warmth is going out of the day, the shadows on the village streets grow longer.

— Her boyfriend is the only one of that lot with a job.

— What does he do?

— He works nights at the service station. Sells people cigarettes and toilet paper at four in the morning.

Marek drives them there before they go back to the

farm, tells Ewa he has a delivery to make, that it won't take long. He parks on the side of the forecourt between the office and the air pressure point and Ewa waits in the car while he goes into the shop. She recognizes the sign, a fat blue lozenge glowing against the pale evening sky. The same company that wanted to open a petrol station in her town but changed their mind. The blank, clean lines seem strangely out of place after the cobbles and crumbling gables of the town square, the comfortable shabbiness of the buildings on the farm. Here the road is new asphalt, and the petrol station is set at a junction, a short distance out of the town, as if they were aware of the clash, wanted to minimize its impact.

The streetlights are coming on, the forecourt lights too. Marek comes out of the shop with a laughing German man and they start unloading the boot. Ewa gets out to help them, piles the boxes of dog food and salty biscuits behind the door to the forecourt office. The German shakes Marek's hand, then passes him a neat roll of notes, fastened with a rubber band.

Marek fills up the tank and then waves, one arm reaching through the open window as they drive out onto the road again.

— He's the franchise owner. I got to know him last year.

He made a deal with him to bring a few bits and pieces from Poland, and the dog food has sold very well.

— Artur drove home to see his wife last night and I got him to bring some more back over. His cut should stop him moaning awhile anyway.

Ewa looks across at Marek in the driving seat, thinks he is enjoying his new incarnation, acting the hustler. He smiles and winks at her, and then he shrugs.

— You know Lila, our eldest girl. Wants to be a dental assistant, so she has to take exams. I want to support her.

Marek says they still have a few years. Before Poland joins the EU and smuggling and asparagus harvests are a thing of the past.

— And he will have to look further east for cheaper labor, our farmer. Belarus. Maybe Mongolia.

Marek laughs and Ewa thinks of the Russians who used to come into town selling tortoises and caviar, children's shoes and cigarettes that were all cardboard filter. And Dorota's neighbors who fly to New Delhi in the summer, fill bags with gray acrylic jumpers and stainless steel buckets in the bazaars. Sell them in the winter at the junction of the road to Poznan and the border. Given the choice, Ewa thinks being a dental assistant is preferable.

Three days later, Ana from Warsaw has a message for Ewa when she gets out of the shower.

— There was a call for you.

— My son?

— No. Someone called Marta in Berlin. She has an address for you. Here.

Ewa reads the scribbled note, sits on her bed, and looks for the road on her map. West Berlin this time, and Ewa wonders if she will be able to tell the difference. She finds the nearest underground station. *Schlesisches Tor.* Silesia: where she is from, and Piotr. And the last stop on the line is called Warschauer Strasse. Warsaw. Ewa points this out to Ana, then Adela, who laughs.

— He tries, but he can't get away from us, can he?

It pours overnight and the guttering on the barn overflows, rivulets seeping in under the door in the early hours, deep puddles forming under the sorting tables inside. Ewa doesn't go out to the fields straightaway, mops the barn instead with the farmer and his wife. She listens to them argue quietly as they work. About money, from what she can gather, her few German words. Ewa empties the buckets in the yard and they stand by the door together, silent now, squinting up at the damp brickwork and rusting pipes. The roof is sagging in places, the paintwork on the farmhouse hasn't been done in years. Ewa feels she is seeing the place with new eyes, but watching the tight, disappointed gestures of the farmer's wife, she is sure that none of this has escaped her notice.

The farmer calls her over before she makes her way out to the fields.

— We have some clients in the city where we deliver personally, restaurants and shops. I'll be going on Saturday; if you want, you can drive in with me.

— Thank you.

Ewa doesn't ask how he knows she wants to go back to Berlin. Would rather not hear who has been gossiping. He holds out his hand to shake, says his name, his first name, which Ewa doesn't quite understand, but she thinks it sounds like Gerhard, although she doesn't like to ask him to repeat himself. His grip is surprisingly light, palm hard and dry.

— I'm Ewa.

Saturday, and the truck is already parked in the yard when Ewa comes out after a late breakfast. The farmer and his daughter are waiting. She climbs up into the cab beside the girl, says hello to her in Russian, but she shakes her head in response, frowning, flushing. The farmer smiles, explains that they have English in school now, and Ewa tries her best accent:

— Good morning.

— Good morning.

The girl replies, polite, but she avoids eye contact, scratches at an imaginary spot on her jeans. Her father smiles over her head at Ewa and drives on.

Ewa tries to work out how old he is: *like Marek*. Teenage children: so most likely in his forties. Remembers she will have a teenage son soon, and then she will be in her thirties. They drive in silence, the van engine too loud for talking. Ewa watches the villages pass, the girl next to her chewing her fingernails. Her family has been farming round here since Napoleon was beaten. When Marek told her that, it seemed an eternity, but now Ewa thinks how brief the generations seem, and the times they live through. Her own grandfather, she knew, had fought with the Germans in the First World War. Piotr's father was born before the second and told her partisan stories from his childhood, tales of heroic uprisings against the Nazis in the nights when Jacek was a baby and kept them awake all the time. She remembers her mother's descriptions of being moved to Silesia, too. After the war: Stalin's orders. How the house they were put in had belonged to a German family before, like so many others in the town. Ewa recalls her mother's descriptions, the Germans leaving on horseback and foot, in tears and anger, walking westward, just as they had done a few weeks before. She said she had cried, too, leaving their old home in the east, crossing the wide waters of the Bug. But her tears had stopped quickly, as soon as she fell in love with the open, unfamiliar landscape.

The farmer drives steadily, the road widens, cars overtake them. Ewa wonders if Marek tells his sons about strikes and solidarity and life in the underground or if he prefers not to. They are out of the countryside now, but not yet in the city. All along the roadside are warehouses, car parks. Places to buy wood, furniture, VCRs, and garden tools. Perhaps the farmer has stories to tell his daughter: about her grandfather's land maybe, about the collectivization and the spirit of 1989, or what the country looked like before there were superstores and DIY. She always liked hearing about the past herself, wonders if the girl next to her does, if she wants to be a farmer at all, or rather a petrol station attendant or a dental assistant.

Ewa doesn't tell Jacek stories. Realizes she has never tried, and now that she thinks about it, she is not sure what she has to say. *We wanted it to change and then it did.* Not much else comes to mind. She says:

— I hated Russian lessons. German, English are much more useful.

A statement out of nothing after such a long silence, and Ewa can see in the wing mirror that she is blushing.

The farmer drops her at an underground station, and she rattles along the dark blue line until she can change to the green and make her way to Piotr's neighborhood. The train runs on elevated tracks above the traffic, level with the windows in the flats that line the wide city street. Balconies full of flowers and bicycles, graffiti, peeling paintwork. The stations are announced in a calm, automated voice: Ewa gets out one stop early and walks. Dark-haired, dark-eyed children play on the streets; women stand in small groups laughing, wearing head scarves, long coats, and Ewa can't understand what they say, but it doesn't sound like German. Arabic, Turkish, perhaps: In the shop windows there are half-moons and stars, red Turkish flags.

Ewa finds a café, orders by pointing at one of the large bowls of milky coffee being drunk at the next table. After the waitress has gone she worries about how much it will cost, and finds a menu, tries to read it. Thinks she recognizes the word and that she will have to pay a fair amount of what she has in her pocket, but still she is not certain. Wonders how Piotr managed; if he can speak German now, how quickly he learned it. Last time she was here she got by without speaking to anyone. When Adela was in Krakow, she had a boyfriend who works on a building site here now. She says he's been in Berlin two years and can't speak a word. Doesn't need to, stays amongst his own, the legions of legal-illegal Polish men rebuilding the old-new capital.

Ewa thinks, this was West Berlin, and that it doesn't look so different from the area she was in last time she came. But then Paula had told her this is where all the hippies and immigrants live. Go out to the suburbs, she said, endless houses with double garages, that's the real Berlin-West. Ewa opens her map out on the table, finds where she is now, where she was two weeks ago, figures the river must be somewhere behind the houses over her left shoulder. Already some things are familiar, the sound of the yellow trains, the warm damp-and-bread smell in the underground stations. The high tenements, uneven paving on the roads, small children sitting on bicycle seats in front of their parents. She can see why people like it here, why Piotr would want to stay, but he couldn't have known about any of this before, so it doesn't explain why he came.

Four names on the buzzer, none of them Piotr's, none of them even Polish. But this is the second floor, just as Marta had directed, the door on the right as you come up the stairs. She wonders as she rings the bell whether Marta may have warned him. Your wife came to see me. You never said you had a kid.

After the bell there is quiet, and Ewa experiences a brief moment of panic. But then come footsteps and there is no time left for worry or doubt. The door is open and just inside is a face, both familiar and unfamiliar.

— Hello.

— Ewa.

— Hello.

A little fatter, this face, softer, hair a little longer. It makes Ewa's throat ache. Piotr looks tired. He wears jeans and T-shirt, slippers, and his hands are damp, covered in suds.

— Can I come in?

Ewa smiles, her mouth, throat, chest hurt. Piotr doesn't say anything or move, and Ewa is aware of how calm she must seem, stepping past him into the hallway, where a vacuum cleaner stands plugged in, hose discarded on the floor beside it. The kitchen door is open and she can see dishes piled high on the side, soapy water in the sink, and above it a clock showing ten past three. Ewa tries swallowing, to shift the ache a little lower. There seems endless space down there for it to occupy. She can feel herself drifting a little, there in the hall. The motorway journey in the loud van, she thinks, or maybe this hollow body feeling is what you get seeing your husband again after such a long time.

He has not shaved. The stubble on his chin is darker than his hair, more red than blond, and stronger than she remembers. When he left he had just turned twenty-three. Strange to think that his body has been changing, thickening, aging, when he is still so young. Her hair color has changed many times over the years, thanks to Dorota, but Ewa thinks there must be other new things about her, and perhaps Piotr can see them. She turns to check, and he is looking at her. She blinks.

— You got my letters, Ewa?

That empty-ache feeling again.

— I got three letters from your lawyer. The papers.

— You have them with you now?

— No. I don't.

The flat is large. Ewa counts four rooms off the wide hallway, and there is a corridor at the far end which leads round a corner. Piotr sees her looking.

— It's just me at home. The others are working.

Ewa waits, but he doesn't say who the others are. Friends, flatmates, lovers.

— You're cleaning.

— It's my turn. Do you want coffee?

When they were younger, they spent their summers at the river. Always, from May to September. The last one was after Jacek was born, and Piotr would join them there in the evenings, after he finished working. Animated talk on the riverbank with friends, the election results debated and celebrated under the late summer sun. Cigarettes and dry-sour red wine from Bulgaria; old tractor inner tubes inflated, floated out onto the slow-flowing water; she and Piotr lying together, feet and hands dipping into the river; drifting through the cool evenings; Jacek, their long baby boy, lying across their bellies.

Ewa remembers this now, in Piotr's Berlin kitchen. Thinks that was the last time when they were really together. The last time when everything seemed possible: The wall dividing this city had not yet fallen, but in their country, things were already moving.

Two years later he was gone. Was it just not fast enough for him?

Piotr stands when he hears the key in the door, hands hovering, eyes fixed on the hallway, and Ewa has to resist the urge to stand as well when she hears a German voice call.

— Hello! It's me. Piotr?

— Here.

He is at the kitchen door already, before the woman in the hallway has called his name. She steps into view, holds out an arm to him in greeting, and now Ewa stands, too. She is a little taller than Piotr, long dark hair loose, tucked behind her ears. Her face is broad and clear, she is smiling, and tries not to stop when Piotr introduces them.

— Nicole, Ewa, Nicole.

No explanations. Ewa smiles back at the German woman, but none of them can find a way to break the silence which follows. Ewa can smell the coffee boiling on the stove, the washing-up water; the cool smell of the afternoon outside which the German woman has brought in with her. She hears her ask Piotr out into the hall.

Their voices stay low and calm, and it is brief, their conversation. Ewa doesn't know what they say to each other, but she sees how the flush spreads across the skin on the German woman's neck. Shocking red. How she puts a hand up to cover it. *Nicole.*

She doesn't look at Piotr as he pulls his jacket on, turns away and walks into one of the rooms off the hallway. Ewa is still standing in the kitchen, sees Nicole disappear, hears the door closing. Piotr takes hold of Ewa's elbow and then they are out in the stairwell, and down, at the front door. He looks straight ahead, walks fast, crosses one road, and then another. Ewa has to jog to keep up.

— Where are we going?

He doesn't answer immediately.

— I don't know.

He drops his pace. They come to a corner, a junction with the wide road where the traffic runs on either side of the elevated railway. They walk along more slowly, following the line of the tracks with the sun behind them. Late afternoon, cool but clear; shopkeepers pack away their crates of aubergines and apples, people sit outside the pavement cafés with their coats on, faces turned to the sun's last rays.

Piotr starts a few explanations. He wants to study; he will have to save some money, but thinks it might be possible here. Bicycle bells ring them to the other side of the pavement and they jump into line, walk in single file for a while. Piotr ahead, Ewa aware of the paving stones beneath her shoes, the gritty feel of the pale dusting of sand, just as she'd imagined. The walkway widens again, Piotr drops back beside her.

— What do you want to be, then?

— A nurse. For old people, I think. I'm not quite sure yet.

He looks uncomfortable, Ewa doesn't know why. Perhaps because she is surprised.

— I did some work like that before, I was good at it, I think. It's how I met Nicole. I worked for her family, took care of her grandfather until he died.

Piotr frowns and Ewa is aware now that she is staring at him. She looks at the path ahead.

— Sorry.

A nurse. Not what she had expected; but it is a good idea, sensible. At home, he'd worked at the factory, like so many others, until it closed. She had never thought to ask him what he actually wanted to do. Be with her, is what she'd presumed. And Jacek. She asks:

— What do you do now?

He avoids eye contact.

— You're not working?

— I was. But Nicole. It's illegal and she doesn't want me to get caught, get sent back.

— So she supports you.

— Just for now.

Ewa is quiet. All the restaurants they pass have chalkboards outside, and it's written all over them. *Spargel, spargel.* Asparagus, asparagus. With potatoes and butter. Wrapped in bacon. German asparagus with Italian ham. Some even have the name of the village on them, the farm where she is working.

— She's a teacher.

Grew up here, he says, in the east of the city, works in a primary school in one of the western suburbs.

— Let's eat something. You can buy me dinner.

Ewa is surprised at herself, her tone of voice, but Piotr doesn't argue, just finds them a table outside on the wide pavement, under the trees. It is busy and the waiter ignores them, so Piotr gets up to fetch a menu and Ewa looks up and around. The branches above her are thick with leaves, the heavy smell of their greenish blossom. The elevated track runs behind them and Ewa catches yellow flashes: glimpses of color as a train passes. She watches the carriages tilt and slow as the tracks follow the curve of the road. She is not sure what she wants to say to Piotr now and thinks, briefly, about leaving, getting on one of the overhead trains, then out of the city. But Piotr is back, with bottles of beer from inside, and a menu, which he starts to translate for Ewa.

— It's okay, I know what I want. Asparagus.

— Yes?

— I've been cutting it for weeks, I want to eat some.

— It's good here. They cook it well. With potatoes is best, traditional.

— You come here a lot?

— Sometimes.

She thinks about his modest life, his shy girlfriend. Qualification, a steady career path, a reasonable apartment, the occasional meal in a mid-price restaurant. It doesn't seem so different from lives led in Krakow, Gdansk,

Wrocław; not so different from the life she wants, either, with the exception that he sees his life without her. *Things have improved at home, you know, since you left us*, she wants to object, but so much about him is different, so much she hadn't expected, that Ewa feels her protest vanish, even before she's made it. Just like her country, she thinks: trying hard but still left behind somehow. *Is that how he sees it?* She doesn't want to cry, can't even feel angry. Thinks maybe that will all come later, and the thought is a little frightening.

— And Jacek is fine?

Ewa thinks she can hear the answer he wants in his question.

— Yes, he's fine.

She waits, but Piotr doesn't seem to have more to ask about their son, and so Ewa talks to cover the silence, her disappointment.

— He does well in school. Doesn't work hard enough, but he's clever. A bit wild sometimes, but I like that. I didn't bring a photo. Sorry.

— That's okay.

Piotr takes a sip of his beer, looks at her across the table.

— I'll send you money for him, Ewa. Soon as I start earning.

He holds eye contact; the promise is sincere but the moment uncomfortable. Ewa picks up her beer and drinks too. The ache in her throat is back and she wants to swallow it. She needs the money, of course, but to Ewa the promise feels like second best, humiliation. Not what she came for.

She doesn't say anything, can only think how Dorota will react when she tells her: a sarcastic demand, probably, for Piotr's statement in writing. And then their food comes, and with it a moment's grace to think of a response, while the waiter lays the plates on the table. *Be pragmatic, be like Dorota.* Ewa calculates: This meal will cost about the same as a week's rent, and if Piotr sends them that every month, she and Jacek can move, and she won't have to sleep in the kitchen. But then the waiter says he is changing shifts and could they please pay up front, and Piotr takes so long to find enough to cover the bill, searching through his pockets, that Ewa abandons her pragmatics again. Pushes at the long white spears on her plate instead, picks up her fork and crushes a potato. She doesn't look at Piotr. Doesn't move to try her own pockets, knows she has just about enough for the train fare back in borrowed money. She will not tell Dorota about this, says to herself, *Doesn't matter, doesn't matter, doesn't matter.* They have got by so far without him, and it will just have to go on that way.

She thinks about Feliksa, wonders if she ever doubted Marek would return and what that felt like. Wonders how she will feel back in Poland knowing that Piotr will not come home. At the moment she tastes the smooth asparagus fibers, the salty butter, the floury potatoes.

— You will marry her, then?

The waiter has gone.

— Yes.

— For the papers?

He shrugs. Above them, beyond the trees, a train is coming. Slow metal jolt and groan, Ewa has to raise her voice as it approaches.

— It's not that way for her, is it?

— No.

— For you?

No words, just a small movement of the head.

Ewa listens as the train rolls over them, passes. Thinks she should be pleased: He is trying his best not to hurt her. That it is funny: that after all the years and everything in them, he should want to be so careful.

Nicole is still awake when they come back to the flat. The light is not on in the hallway, but Ewa can see she has been crying.

— Would you like to stay? Please stay, it is no problem.

She is learning Polish, she says, speaks hesitantly, correctly. The words come out slow, but they are friendly. Nicole gathers sheets and blankets, pulls the couch cushions together on the floor, brings a pillow through from their bedroom. Ewa waits by the window, realizes when the bed is made that she never offered to help her.

— T-shirt? Something to sleep in?

— I'll be fine. Thank you.

The flat is quiet, the curtains open. Ewa lies on the floor and watches as the occasional car headlights pass across the ceiling. When it gets light she washes her face and leaves the blankets folded on the sofa.

The station is not far, so she walks to save the waiting and the bus fare, and once there, she finds a bench, lies half awake on the clean, new platform.

Changes are coming, always more of them, but their lives are passing too. Too fast to be waiting. Jacek will be grown one day soon, and that whole part of her life over. Unless she finds another man, has another baby, begins again with a whole new family. Or she could study, maybe with Lila, maybe if Piotr really does start earning and sending them money. Or she will talk to her sister. About training and then working for her in the salon. Not sure what Tadeusz would say to that, but it's what Dorota always wanted.

Ewa dozes. Doesn't know what all these plans will look like when she gets home. Doesn't want to think about that now. Not about Piotr or Nicole or anything for a while.

When the kiosk opens she counts out her change, buys a coffee, a pretzel. The station roof is high and light, trains and announcements more frequent now. Seven-thirty-five and the first train out is not till after nine. At the farm they will be finishing their breakfast; by midmorning she will be out in the fields again. Two more weeks, three at the most, then home. Ewa thinks she will wait another half hour, then go and find a phone.

Jacek will just be awake by then, and she looks forward to hearing the rhythm of sleep still in his breathing, his sullen morning tones.

ACKNOWLEDGMENTS

Grateful thanks to Toby Eady and his Associates, and to all at Orme Court. To my editors Ravi Michandani, Georg Reuchlein, Claudia Vidoni, and especially Dan Frank. To Willy Maley for always having time. Also to the many people who helped me in the research and writing: Agnieszka Latakos, Siobhan Edwards, Paddy Lyons, Paul Welsh, Gretchen Seiffert, Hedi Röhl, Gertrud Waageman, Harald Heinrich in Beelitz, Dieter Tannenberger of the Dachverband der privaten Bauernverbände in Dittmannsdorf, Herr Nienhaus from the Landesarbeiteramt in Berlin, Terry Thomas and his bees, and the British Beekeepers Association.

ABOUT THE AUTHOR

Rachel Seiffert's first novel, *The Dark Room*, was short-listed for the Booker Prize and won a Betty Trask Award and the *L.A. Times* first novel prize. She was chosen as one of Granta's Best of Young British Novelists, and her stories have won a David Wong Award from PEN International. She has lived in Glasgow and Berlin, and now lives in London with her husband and new son.